# CYCLE

# CYCLE

K. R. FERGUSON

Ferg House Classics

# Contents

# I

# Acknowledgement

To my husband Paul, your unwavering support is the source of my comfort and encouragement. In moments that I don't believe in myself, you are my greatest cheerleader. You are my rock, my confidant, and my greatest ally. I couldn't imagine doing life with anyone but you. To my best friends Jes and Amanda, from the inception of this project to the final word on the page, your support, creative insights, and collaborative spirits have been nothing short of extraordinary. Amanda, you were the first to lay eyes on this book and the first round of edits it went through. From the first chapter through graphics, thank you for investing your time and efforts in helping me make this dream a reality. Jes, this book would not exist without you. You planted the seeds of becoming an author as you sat and listened to me tell you about a wild dream that I had. Even after blowing you off, you continued to encourage me sentence by sentence, chapter by chapter. You spent countless hours reading, re-reading, and listening to my ramblings to transform a dream into physical form. Thank y'all for being my sounding board and a constant source of inspiration.

# 2

# Hailey

Ten years doesn't seem to be a long time when you are doing things you love. Ten years worth of vacations, Christmas', birthdays embraced in all of life's joys will pass like a whisper. But ten years on the run? Those birthdays, holidays and joyous occasions all missed become a ghost of what could have been. The smiles and laughter that should have filled those years echo as distant shadows instead. Two thirds of my life has been stolen, replaced by a journey where my survival eclipses the joys of existence. We have been on the run for so long, that I find myself looking over my shoulder wondering if I would even recognize the men after me at this point. With their faces carved into my nightmares, the irony isn't lost on me. Ten years of waking up covered in a sheath of cold sweat as I ground myself back to reality should have etched their familiarity, but instead, I'm plagued by the question of whether they have changed as much I have. I've grown up. I'm no longer a blonde hair, blue eyed five year old who is able to look at the world through rose colored glasses. They made sure of that when they broke into our house that night. My heart yearns for a sliver of anonymity, a desperate hope that their memory of me is a faded snapshot distorted by the passage of time. But as much as I want to believe that they wouldn't be able to recognize me, I would also have to acknowledge that the very people who haunt me have become elusive phantoms, that line between predator and pray blurring as they transform into faceless entities. That thought alone is scarier than knowing that there are people out there who want me dead.

As I lay cocooned in my bed, the scent of bacon wafts down the hall and into my room, and I know my aunt is making breakfast. The smells coming from the kitchen should be inviting, but instead they carry a weight, an unspoken reminder of the days significance. Today is a day that I should be celebrating, yet I dread it every year. Birthdays should be a joyous occasion. After all, how many fifteen year old kids do you know who don't enjoy their birthday? But this day, my day, doesn't represent another year around the sun. Instead, it's tainted by another narrative. Today marks another year since my life was ripped away from me. Another day that my memories continue to fade and elude me. I close my eyes and try so hard to remember what my mom looked like, what she smelled like, her smile, her infections laugh, anything about her. But just like yesterday, and all the days before, no matter how hard I try, I can't. It's as if they're fading, slipping into the abyss that separates me from my former life. Frustrated with myself, I throw off my duvet, its purple fabric a fleeting sanctuary of warmth, and head to my closet to get dressed for the day.

Like every year, Aunt Kat will let me skip school. I think she must know how hard today is for me, but she never brings it up. On any normal day, our house buzzes with frenetic energy. Pop-tarts are scarfed down and backpacks grabbed in haste, as we tumble of out of the door in a whirlwind of morning chaos in an attempt to not be late. But not today. Today everything shifts. Today, she'll make a big breakfast, slyly ask me if I want to skip school, and then go on to tell me about some elaborate plan that she has made, her words not carrying the weight of today. Not once will she mention my birthday, and for a second I find myself wondering if she knows how much I appreciate that. I stop with my fingers suspended over the hanger that my favorite pink camisole hangs from and remind myself that I should probably hear what she has planned before settling on an outfit. Although it's April, and Texas is in it's pre-summer warm up where the temperature hovers around eighty degrees and you feel like you can drown from the humidity in the air when you walk outside. Memories of our prior escapades begin to filter through my mind. Last year she flew us to New York for a four day weekend. For the most part I had packed shorts, with only a single pair of jeans, and zero long sleeved shirts. When we got off the plane the weather app on her phone dinged, alerting us that the temperature high would be fifty-three degrees. Immediately we knew that would be ill prepared for the weekend ahead. To ward off the chilly weather we were sure to face, we purchased some I heart NY hoodies from the airport gift shop, anticipating that their fleece would become an armor against the cold air. What we didn't expect though, was how windy it would be, and its powerful gusts unmatched ability to make us feel like we were freezing from the inside out. We ended up having to buy four days worth of clothes and we were still miserable. A chill makes its way down my spine at the vivid memory. Before I can give it another thought, I hear the high pitched scream of the smoke detector going off and Aunt Kat cussing from the kitchen. I can't help but smile to myself at her explicit words painting a picture of the chaos I am sure is unfolding. Aunt Kat is a lot of things, but a chef is not one of them.

As I'm walking down the hall, I hear the front door open, and the deep bass of Sam's voice echo through the house.

"Are you cooking breakfast, or trying to burn down the house?"

The loud sigh that emanates from Aunt Kat as a response matches perfectly to the deflated expression that is plastered on her face as I round the corner into the smoke filled kitchen. The moment that she spots me, her expression changes and turns into a beaming smile.

"Good morning Sweetie! I'm so sorry, did the smoke alarm wake you?"

"No ma'am, I was already up. What's going on?"

Both Sam and I find ourselves drawn to the spectacle before us, silent witnesses to the comedy unfolding as she feverishly swings a dish towel over her head at the smoke detector in an attempt to get the alarm to stop blaring. The stool that she is standing on leaves no room for error. It's a delicate balancing act, a tightrope walk between putting out the alarm and a more disastrous ending. If she leans too much one way, or moves her feet at all, we're going to have bigger problems on our hands than just a little smoke. Just when it appears like she is going to give up, the screeching stops, and with a triumphant exhale she steps down from the stool. Her kinky onyx hair is even more disheveled than usual sitting in a messy bun just off to the left side of her head. With one hand on her hip, and the towel still in the other, she spins around and chuckles.

"Well, I *was* cooking breakfast for us, but you see how well that's going. What do you say we catch breakfast at the diner instead?"

"What, no pop tarts for breakfast this morning?" Sam interjects with a grin.

The death glare Aunt Kat gives him doesn't go unnoticed by either of us. Ignoring him and redirecting her eyes to me she continues.

"Hailey, what do you say about skipping school today? I already have the day off, and I was thinking we could do something fun. We can drive down to Galveston and hit up the pier, maybe ride some rides? Or since it's Friday, we can make it a long weekend, fly to Florida and spend some time at a real beach!"

As anticipated, the conversation unfolds along familiar lines. There's a comfort in the predictability of her attempt to make today special without acknowledging what day it is, and I hold a silent appreciation for her subtlety. However, I'd give my left arm to do nothing and just sleep through the day for once. The thought of soft white sand between my toes and crystal clear water for miles has me giving Florida a second thought. With all the traveling that we've done, the only beach that I've gone to is Galveston. With it's muddy brown waters and sand that reminds me of the mud pies that I made in my sandbox when it rained as a kid, Florida is tempting.

"Can we just stay at home? I can go back to bed and catch up on sleep. Then maybe we can order a pizza in later or something."

My aunt's face falters for a split second, and had I not been looking directly at her in that brief moment, I would have missed the fleeting look that she gave Sam. It's as if they have some secret that I'm not in on. But just as fast as it was there, it went away and my aunt's smile returns in its place.

"What was that?" I questioned.

"What was what?"

"That look you just gave Sam."

"I don't know what look you're talking about."

I don't know if I should be more irritated with the fact that she scoffed at me with that statement, or at that she's lying to my face.

"You just looked at Sam like you had something to say, but couldn't say it in front of me. By all means please share the secret with the crowd!"

My voice registers in a pitch higher and much louder than I intend, but this isn't the first time that I have seen them share a look, or a whisper, when they thought that I wasn't looking or listening. A memory resurfaces of the first time I caught them, an indiscernible look shared in the fleeting shadow of a moment. I had just turned eight, and we had moved here a few months prior. Sam was our neighbor and for a long time I thought that they were secretly dating, or maybe I just hoped they were. In my old life, it was always just my mom and I. My dads absence was palpable, a void left by a man who died before I was born. My mom never liked to talk about him, but his presence lingered through his best friend John Weigle. John was the closest connection that I had to my dad, but his time was limited with responsibilities of a wife and child of his own. My mom never dated anyone, her focus unwavering on raising me. Sam is the closest person to a father figure that I have had. He helped my aunt with child care when I was younger by watching me after school, or on weekends when she had to pick up additional shifts at work. He came to school award programs, and wasn't a stranger at parent-teacher conferences. He picked up wherever my aunt needed help, and was there any time she couldn't be. His involvement was far from obligatory and he became an extension of our lives. He was the first, and so far the only person that my aunt has seemed to trust since starting our new life. I never found it odd, or questioned it, until recently.

In the past six months or so, I have noticed a subtle shift in their interactions, an influx of hushed whispers and fleeting glances between the two of them. Part of me can feel the shift, as if there's a physical divide between the before and the now. I don't know what could have caused the riff or why now, but something causes the hairs on the back of my neck to stand up, and the ball of anxiety that I live with to drop into the pit of my stomach during moments like these. I can feel the anxiety building as I go down the rabbit hole of 'what ifs?'. My hands, once steady, turn clammy and a prickly sensation starts to unfurl, like a spider tracing its way across my skin. It inches its way from limb to limb until every inch of my body is tingling with its presence. An invisible vice begins to tighten inside of me, the pressure building in my stomach and clawing its way upward into my chest. If I continue on this path, I have no doubt that Monster inside of me will wake from its slumber and take over. It will creep up my throat, gripping me with its invisible hand, keeping oxygen from entering or exiting my lungs. I won't be able to breathe. From one moment to the next, my body is no longer my own. With its jaws snapping at the edges of my composure, I begin to involuntarily shake, first inwardly, until the Monster takes over with such force that my hands, arms, and legs begin to tremble. Its roar resonates in my ears drowning out the world around me as it takes center stage in my mind, body and soul . My surroundings fade away leaving only the sound of my heart to fill the void. My vision narrows, the edges dimming as if reality itself is withdrawing, leaving me alone in a tunnel of encroaching darkness. The abyss looms along the black edges, threatening to consume me and swallow me whole. I know this is going to end in one of two ways. Either I'm going to throw up, or pass out. Sometimes I get a double dose, and both happen. I'm no stranger to panic attacks and neither throwing up or passing out are the way I want to spend the day, so rather than surrender to the impending doom, I cling to the last shreds of rationality.

In the battle between panic and reason, I wrestle to gain control. There is no way that she told him anything. Not anything true anyways. So these whispers and looks can't be about us, right? They can't be about our past life, the people after me, what she is, or how we got here. They can't possibly signify that some table in the universe has turned and that we will be back to running soon, or worse, we'll be found.

Had she told him, he would have gone running for the hills, or maybe reported her to the police for being a crazy person. After all, no sane person would believe our story, and he certainly wouldn't have stuck around after being told the truth, much less willingly be standing in our kitchen having a conversation about burnt bacon, right? I can feel the Monster begin to retreat as the quiver in my stomach starts to ease, the internal earthquake calming. As my vision begins to return, my white-knuckled grip on the counter top slowly relaxes, my muscles uncoiling with each passing second. A touch, heavy yet gentle, lands on my shoulder sending a jolt through my body, attempting to pull me back into the present.

"Hailey... kid, you okay?"

A distorted voice pierces through the the sensations swirling within my head, a flicker of a sound barely discernible above the whooshing sounds that are pulsating in my ears and match the rhythm of my heartbeat. Concentrating harder on the voice, it grows louder and as the ringing in my ears recedes, and I recognize it as Sam's from what seems like miles away, even though he's standing right next to me. Desperately inhaling a deep breath, I turn and spin around facing away from Sam and my aunt concealing the rage of embarrassment that is building within me. It's bad enough that I nearly had a complete meltdown today of all days, but for it to be witnessed by the only two people I have left in this world is unacceptable. The idea of their eyes filled with sympathy, or worse, pity is not something that I can bare to see. Had I turned around in that moment and come face to face with it, I would have completely lost it. So instead, without saying a word, I stomp off to my room and slam my door. The familiarity of my bed calls to me, a haven where I can reclaim a semblance of control over my spiraling thoughts. Quickly crawling in, its layers of fabric serve as a barrier shielding me from the outside world as hot tears fall down my face and silent prayers drift through my thoughts, praying that they leave me alone.

# 3

# Kat

I'm still reeling from the emotional outburst that Hailey just displayed when Sam's voice interrupts my thoughts.

"I guess it's safe to assume that you still haven't talked to her yet."

It wasn't a question; it was a statement, and one that I have been evading. He's right. I haven't told her. The weight of the unspoken words grow heavier with each passing year, a conversation differed but never forgotten. At first, she was too young, her innocence a barrier between her and the harsh truths of the world. No five year old could have possibly understood what was happening, or why a group of grown men are relentless in their pursuit of her. As she matured, it became easier to continue the pretense, to maintain the facade of a normal life while we remained on the run. She never questioned why we always traveled on her birthday, and her face lit up while her eyes sparkled with wonder at all the new sights. At first, all we needed was a day trip, a shift in scenery. We didn't even need to leave the state that we were in, just the city. We could submerse ourselves in a larger city and seek solace in the anonymity the busy crowds provided. When we lived in Washington, we drove to Seattle to see the space needle the day she turned six. She turned seven while we were living in Nevada, so we drove to Las Vegas to ride roller coasters and see shows. But the beacon within her grew stronger, its intensity necessitating more elaborate plans to shield her from our pursuers. I found myself having to plan trips further away and for longer periods of time. A weekend in San Francisco at ten, a three-day excursion to Atlanta at twelve. Last year when she turned fourteen, we took a four day trip to New York, and even with the busy bustle of the city, one of the men still found us. Hailey seemed oblivious to how close we were to being captured, so I never said anything to her. Hindsight being what it is, maybe I should have.

Often I found myself wondering if she even remembered that night, or if she had somehow blocked those memories out. But a few months before she turned eight was when the dreaded question came up on why we had to keep moving. I couldn't bear to look her in the eyes and confess the truth, so I lied. I told her that she was right, it was unfair to her that we moved so often. Then I did the only thing I could think of, I went back to a place of comfort. I moved us to the southern coven, where I knew Sam would be, and where I could hopefully call on his help if I needed it. It was risky, sure, but I didn't know what else to do. Exhaustion had already begun to takes its toll with nearly three years on the run and eight more looming ahead. I thought that her curiosity would unravel a series of inquiries, but her response was unexpected. She was so happy about getting to settle down in what she called a "real home", that she skipped off, curls bouncing behind her and she started to pack. A sense of relief swept over me when she didn't even mention how close Houston was to Louisiana when I revealed where we would be moving. In fact, it was the only time she had ever questioned anything until today. For all the years of deception and evasion, today marks a rupture, a fissure that opens to reveal the truths I've kept hidden. The facade, the unspoken questions, all rise to the surface, ignited by a single question that threatens to dismantle the fortress of half-truths I've built around us.

"No Sam, I haven't."

"If I can sense her, you know they can too. Y'all have to get out of here before it's too late. If you don't, the moment that barrier opens, they are going to be breaking down your door to get her. Not some door in Chicago or Atlanta, but here, your home. You know if that happens it will never be safe for y'all here again. They won't just burn the city down looking for her, they will burn down the entire state until they find her."

"I KNOW!" I yell before catching myself. I take a deep breath,reset, and lower my voice so she doesn't over hear us I start again, "I know. You don't have to tell me what will happen. Don't you think out of all people, I would be the one to understand the consequences? I was the one who was there ten years ago. Not you Sam. Me! I was the one who lost my best friend that night in New Orleans. Trust me when I say that I know what is at stake."

"Then why haven't you told her? She needs to be able to protect herself Katherine."

Frustrated with him, myself, and the entire situation I begin to pace. The kitchen is small, and with Sam's large frame standing in the middle of it, there isn't much room for movement, so I do the next best thing and open the small window above the sink. Walking around Sam I move into the living room, where I open the two windows in there. Our home isn't big, so the cross draft should be enough to get the smoke out from my failed attempt at cooking breakfast, without opening the front or back doors. Sam doesn't say anything, instead he just stands there glaring at me with his piercing blue eyes, waiting on a response. Standing at six foot five and an easy two hundred and fifty pounds of pure muscle, his presence can be intimidating. I know that he thinks I underestimate the seriousness of this and the ramifications of getting caught. He may be leader of the coven for our region and the most powerful warlock in existence, but ironically, it's him that doesn't understand. I've known from the moment that Hailey and I skipped timelines, what needs to be done. Sam doesn't know everything that happened. When we arrived in Houston and gave notice of our presence, he insisted on meeting his new residents. I didn't give any indication that we were anything other than a witch and her human niece prior to meeting. However, I underestimated his abilities and knowledge. He knew the moment that he met us that I hadn't been fully forthcoming with the truth. He could tell that I had strong powers by the aura surrounding my beacon, so I opened up about my chronokinesis in hopes that he would lay off his line of questions. I explained that

Hailey was my best friends daughter, and gave a spin off of what happened back in New Orleans. Giving him a version that it was a random break in, and once they felt Hailey's power, they became obsessed with coming after her. I went on to explain that moving through time was the only way to keep her safe, and refused to indulge what year we came from to avoid compromising her safety any further.

Each witch, wizard, and warlock radiates an aura of energy that we refer to as beacons. The strength of it and how far it reaches ties directly to how strong their powers are. Because of my ability to manipulate time, my beacon is stronger and can be felt for two hundred miles or so. Sam's on the other hand can be felt multiple states away from where he is. At the time, even though Hailey was just shy of eight, her beacon far superseded mine, and would only continue to grow each year. Sam could sense her powers and so this seemed to pacify him. Luckily for us, he didn't know what she was, and I had no intentions on telling him. When he asked about her father, I explained that he had died in an accident just after her mom found out that she was pregnant. I went on further to say that I knew nothing about him but I suspected it is where Hailey's powers came from, as her mom was a mere human. The white lies and half truths have paid off throughout the years. We've made it this far and are so close to the finish line that I can't let anything get in the way now. Sam isn't a patient man and I hope that if I wait him out long enough, he'll drop the conversation. Luckily I don't have to wait long before I hear his heavy sigh and see him rake his hand through his thick brown hair.

"Look, it's almost seven thirty. I've got some stuff to catch up on. What time was she born again?"

"Six oh six in the evening."

I can see him doing the math in his head as he chews on the inside of his lip and nods his head. It's something I've come to note as a habit he does when he's either frustrated or coming to a resolve in a situation.

"Y'all need to be out of here by five. I don't mean at the airport by five, or in the air by five, but on the ground in Florida and hidden by then."

He pulls his phone out of his pocket, and hits a few keys before looking back at me and continuing, "You've got a two and a half hour flight from here to Miami. There's one that takes off at two twenty five. I fully expect y'all to be on that plane or an earlier one. This is non-negotiable Katherine. Protecting that girl is a priority, but so is protecting this city. Last year was a close call, and we don't know how much stronger she'll be this year. I think you should play it safe and not return until Tuesday at the earliest."

My head bobs in a mechanical rhythm, the words spoken by Sam fading into an indistinct drone. Instead all I can think about is how I'm going to get a moody teenager out of the house, on a plane, and safe in a different city for the next five days when I know she's still upset about earlier. The abrupt sound of the front door shutting jolts me back to reality, and I glance around, contemplating my next moves. Abandoning any idea of persuading Hailey to join me for breakfast at the diner, I grab my car keys and head out, hoping that some time apart will allow her to cool down and make the situation more manageable.

Donuts have never let me down, and I'm banking on them to help sweeten the deal as I pull into the local shop. Within fifteen minutes, I've gathered a collection of treats: two donuts adorned with pink sprinkles, one featuring Bavarian cream filling with a smiley face icing on top, and three sausage, egg, and cheese breakfast burritos rest on the passenger seat as I head back towards the house. Living in such a large city like Houston has its pros and cons. It's great that no matter where you live, there is always something that you want near by. Like how we are less than two miles from our closest grocery store, food chains, banks, and any other store we could possibly need. However, the downside is the inevitable traffic that accompanies this convenience, meaning that while we're so close in distance, it's still going to take us at least fifteen minutes to get to any of them. As I pull back into the driveway, having been gone around forty-five minutes, I find myself saying a silent prayer that she has calmed down some and we can get to the airport without a hassle.

The house is quiet when I open the door, so I yell out for Hailey. My voice echoes through the space, and I get no response other than the hum of the air conditioner kicking on. Frowning into the quiet air, I drop my keys in the glass bowl by the garage door, make my way to the kitchen table, and set down the food before trying again.

"I've got donuts! They even had your favorite. You know the Bavarian cream with a smiley face?"

Still nothing but crickets, and a disquieting feeling begins to gnaw at me. Either she's still simmering in resentment over our earlier disagreement, in which case today is destined to be a challenging one, or she's isolating herself with headphones on. I have a sinking feeling that it's the former, so giving it a few more minutes I begin unpacking our breakfast and start to brew coffee. If I'm right, we won't be having breakfast on the go, and there won't be enough caffeine in this house to withstand the conversation that we are about to have. Sam should be happy if we make it to the airport at all, much less on the flight he expects us on. Summoning up every ounce of strength in me, I head down the hall and knock gently on Hailey's door, bracing myself for the potential explosion. Seconds tick by, and nothing comes back. Cautiously, I nudge the door open allowing my head to slip through the gap, hoping to assess the situation inside.

"Hailey?"

When she doesn't answer back, I quietly step in. It's only when the sound of the old floor board creaking under my weight doesn't alert her to my presence, that I realize she's asleep. Knowing we are on a timeline, I lean over her gently shaking her arm, and hold my breath waiting for her to wake.

# 4

# Hailey

*As I play with my dolls in the living room, I can hear the clatter of a metal spoon in a mixing bowl coming from the kitchen as my mom makes a deep purple icing for my cake. The loud chime of the doorbell ringing has me jumping to my feet and yelling "I got it! I got it!" before my mom can even set the bowl down. I'm eager to welcome my best friend, brimming with the anticipation of the birthday games my mom has planned. My steps echo on the floor as I eagerly rush to the front door, my small heart racing with excitement. As the door swings open, my initial excitement gives way to a subtle wave of disappointment. My best friend is not the one standing there. Instead I have to raise my gaze, my eyes tracking up a slim figure before landing on the untamed black locks that I know to be no other than my Aunt Kat. Turning her lips upwards, her smile doesn't quite reach her glowing green eyes. I must not hide my disappointment well, because her smile begins to wane, gradually shifting into a tentative frown.*

*"Why the sad face sweet girl? The birthday girl should never be sad."*

*"I'm not sad. I just thought you were Dean"*

*"Well, I talked to John on my way here, and he said they were running a little late, but promised that they would be here soon."*

*"Mr. Weigle is bringing Dean!"*

*I can't contain my excitement as a small squeal erupts from my throat. John Weigle was my dad's best friend. My mom never talks about my Dad, but John's stories of him are like glimmers of light filling in the gaps and creating memories that feel like cherished secrets shared only with me. Everything that I know about my dad has come from John. Aunt Kat's chuckle pulls my attention back to her.*

*"He sure is. Now how about I turn that frown upside down!"*

*Pulling a large box from behind her back, I can't help but squeal in excitement. I have to stretch my arms as wide as they will go to take the box from her. It's heavy in my small arms, so I hurry over to the spot next to the fireplace that my mom has placed two other bags. I briefly hear my aunt tell my mom that it's six, and the guests will start getting here in the next thirty minutes or so before asking if she needs any help and walks into the kitchen to join her. But my mind is too busy wondering what's in the box to listen to the rest of their conversation. Forgetting about the dolls I left on the floor when the doorbell rang, I begin to play my favorite birthday game 'what's in the bag or box'. Picking up the smaller of the two bags, I start to examine it. It's heavier than I would have expected for its size. Squeezing the bag just enough to feel what's inside, but not so much that it wrinkles, I can tell that whatever is in there is hard, and it fills up the bag completely. A box? It seems silly that my mom would put a box inside of a bag, but unable to figure it out, I move on to the next. This one is bigger, but lighter than the first bag. Taking the same care as I did with the first, I softly begin squeezing it, noting immediately that whatever is inside is soft. A blanket, a pillow, and a stuffed animal are the first things to come to mind. I pause for a second to listen, while I look back towards the kitchen to make sure my mom and aunt are no where in sight, before peeling back the soft white tissue paper to peek inside.*

*A loud clanging noise emanates from the kitchen causing me to jump and shove the bag back in its place, the force of my hand wrinkling the side. With my heart beating hard in my chest, a quick glance around tells me that I'm the only one that was scared by the noise. I quickly turn the bag around, with the wrinkled side facing the wall so that there is no evidence that I touched it showing. I want so desperately to peek back in after seeing a rich purple piece of fabric inside, but don't want to chance getting caught. Instead, I move on to the box that Aunt Kat brought. With its iridescent paper, the color changes from tones of purple, to silvers, pinks, and greens as I move around it to get a better look. Enchanted by its colors, the rest of the world fades away until a pounding knock comes from the front door. Overwhelming excitement overtakes me as I rush to the door to greet my next guest, that I don't stop to wonder why the knock had such force behind it. Or if it was Mr. Weigle and Dean, why they didn't just walk in through the back door like they always do. I don't hear the dishes being dropped in the kitchen or see my aunt rushing towards me as I reach for the door.*

*Suddenly I am no longer standing with my arm stretched up and reaching for the door knob. I'm now standing where the hall meets the living room and watching everything happen from a distance, a third party looking in as the events unfold. The scene begins to play out in slow motion. The younger me is facing away from me, and*

*I can see her blonde curls cascade just past the middle of her back. She has a dainty ribbon tied in a bow holding a small portion of it back that matches the lavender dress she has on. Most kids want themed birthdays of unicorns and mermaids, but not me. Purple is my favorite color and I wanted a purple birthday. I can see the couch covers that my mom sewed from sheets to match the theme when I insisted that everything be purple from where I stand.*

*A sad smile distorts my face, knowing this was my last moment of pure undiluted innocence. I didn't know what terrors and evil the world was made of. I start yelling for the younger me to move, to get away from the door, but she can't hear me. I try running to her to move her, but my feet are cemented to the ground and no matter how hard I struggle to get them to move, they don't budge. I know what's about to happen, and like a train wreck, I can't look away. Aunt Kat comes barreling out of the kitchen with a spatula that's still covered with icing in her hand, but is too far away when the door is kicked in, the red oak splintering throughout the air. I watch as the younger me is hit by the exploding door with such force, that she flies into the air before landing on the glass coffee table, shattering it into a million pieces. I see Aunt Kat change directions towards where I landed, and in that same moment my mom's hand come around the door frame from the kitchen. Just before her head comes around the corner, I see guns come through the front door, and hear them begin to fire, the sound unmistakable.*

*I blink and am teleported back into the body of my younger self, no longer seeing the scene as an outsider, but instead living it. As my vision begins to wane, I see the men breach the doorway. Wearing all black, dressed in cargo pants, boots, and long sleeve turtleneck shirts, not bothering to hide their faces. I don't know how I know this, but instinctively I do. I know that they want us to know who they are, and why they are here. The last thing that I see as I hear my aunt screaming my name, is a man with a faded black tattoo that juts out from the top of his turtle neck shirt and snakes up onto his bald head, lunge for me before my vision plunges into a dark abyss.*

"Hailey... Hailey!"

Bolting upright and breathless, I jump back as I feel the weight of someone else sitting on my bed. Looking around, it takes me a moment to orient my surroundings, when my eyes focus on a familiar face. Aunt Kat's green eyes stand out against her olive skin tone, and in them I can see the worry. We've gone the past decade dodging conversations about our past, but looking at her now, I know that the dreams that continue to haunt me can't be kept a secret anymore. The sympathy that radiates off of her mixed with the pity and worry in her eyes are too much for me to bear. Desperate to look anywhere but at her, I force my head down and focus on my hands in my lap.

"How long?"

The question catches me off guard, and I hesitate before answering. Still unsure of what I may have said out loud while dreaming, and not ready to give up my secrets completely, I cautiously enter the conversation.

"How long what?"

"How long ago did the nightmares start?"

"They've been there since day one."

Her sharp inhale tells me that I've hurt her. I don't mean to, but it's true. I close my eyes and recall that first night. It comes back in a flood of images as clear as the day that it happened.

At first, I didn't remember anything, but nightmare by nightmare, the memories have come back.

*Waking up in a damp and cold room, still wearing my birthday dress, I don't know where I am or how I got here. Listening to my surroundings, I can hear water running. No, not just water, I hear a shower running. Sitting up, my head hurts, but I recognize that I'm in a hotel room. My mom and I have stayed in ones similar. Moving now, I slowly crawl towards the end of the bed and closer to the sound of the shower. Peaking around the corner, the door to the bathroom is closed and I'm immediately face to face with myself in a mirror. Slowly getting off the bed, and walking closer, I see dried blood all over me. I have a large cut on my head that someone has put little white bandages on to hold the gaping edges together. The large cut is surrounded by other small cuts and bruises that are just beginning to show with black and blue hues just under the surface of my skin. Looking down at my arms and legs, I see much of the same. Small and large cuts cover my body, some with similar white bandages on them, and all of which covered in dried blood. My breathing becomes heavy and short. Racking my brain, I try to remember what happened. At first, nothing comes up, but then a memory of gun shots and screams fill my head. My already short breaths become irregular and ragged, each one increasingly harder to breathe in. I start to pull at the collar of my dress to give more room for my chest to expand, but the chiffon material doesn't give at all and the ball of dread that is sitting in my stomach begins to creep its way into my chest.*

*I have to get out of here. It's clear to me that someone hurt me. I am not alone in this hotel room, and only a bathroom door is standing between me and them. I hear the shower water turn off, and the scrape of the metal curtain hooks sliding against the rod. I rush towards the main door, the only means of escape, and yank it open. A loud bang echos in the nearly empty room when the lock at the top of the door catches and it comes to an abrupt stop. I'm too short to reach the lock and looking around there is no chair or anything else in the room that I can stand on to reach it. Desperate to get the door open, I begin to jump with all my might as high as I can, with my arm extended as far as it will go above my head, praying that I can hit the lock. The first jump, I miss. Another jump, and my fingers touch the silver lock just on the underside, but not quite enough to flip the lock open. Stepping back, I take a running jump at it for a third time, and catch the lock just enough for it to move a tiny amount, but not enough for me to open the door. As I'm gearing up for what I hope to be my last jump, the bathroom door behind me swings open. I pivot around as I back myself against the door. The only thing that I can hear is my heartbeat pounding in my head. Why can't I breathe? Why can't I hear anything? Just as my captor steps out of the bathroom, my vision goes dark and I feel myself falling to the floor.*

"Why didn't you say anything?"

The question catches me off guard, and pulls me back from my memories. Instinctively, my fingers reach up to trace the scar just above my right temple. How could I have told her? Aside from the one conversation that she explained things to me, we've never really discussed what happened. I know that she has her own demons that shes battling regarding that night. The choices that she made didn't just affect me, they affected her as well. She was my mom's best friend, which is how she earned the title Aunt Kat. Each choice that she made built up not only to me losing my mom, but her losing her best friend as well. It wouldn't be fair of me to unload my burdens on her, especially when her sacrifices are what have kept me alive all these years. Not to mention, after my panic attack that first night, I promised my five year old self that I would never show weakness to anyone ever again. With nothing to say, I hang my head and shrug my shoulders. The hug comes out of nowhere and takes me aback. It's the type of hug that is fast and hard, and you can tell that they don't want to let go. A few seconds in, I feel something warm make its way down my neck but it's not until I hear the sniffle that comes next, that I know they are tears and that she's crying. It's only as we break apart, that I realize that I'm crying too. It's a strange feeling, letting my guard down like this in front of someone else. It's been an eternity since I last cried in the presence of another person, but despite my inner protest, the hot tears continue to stream down my face.

"I am so sorry that you felt like you needed to do this alone. You could have told me."

Her words make the tears flow faster. Unable to keep up with wiping them away, I pick up my pillow and bury my face in it. It's a silent but forceful cry, the kind that no matter how hard you try to hold in, you can't. The type of cry that leaves you with a pounding headache when it's finished. I'm not sure how long I sit like that, but the soft comfort of a hand rubbing my back has me lifting my head and looking towards my aunt.

"Come on, I've got some donuts in the kitchen. I made some coffee too, although it might be cold by now. I have a feeling we're going to need all the sugar and caffeine for this conversation."

Without saying another word, she gets up and walks out

of my door and down the hall. I think about getting dressed before going out there, but I don't have the energy. So instead, I reach over to the post of my bed that I keep my hair ties on and grab my favorite gray scrunchie. Throwing my hair up and getting it out of my face, I stand and follow in tow as I listen for the buttons of the microwave being pushed.

# 5

# Hailey

Stepping into the kitchen, the aroma of fresh coffee and the sight of the carefully arranged breakfast treats on the table invite a flutter of warmth into my heart. The spread is like a visual hug, with my favorite Bavarian cream donut right in the middle, smiling up at me with yellow and black frosting on top. Grabbing it and a napkin, I sit down in the chair to the left and watch as my aunt pulls one cup of coffee from the microwave, replacing it with the other and hitting the quick minute button. Our table isn't big, and as she walks over with my cup, I find myself having to shift some of the food around to make room. Waiting for my aunt to sit down, I bite into my donut, savoring the initial crunch as a symphony of flavors unfolds in my mouth. The soft cream melds seamlessly with the delicate sweetness of the pastry, and I can't help but close my eyes momentarily. Opening my eyes as the microwave chirps indicating that it's done, I see the time on the stove. How is it nine o'clock already? Had I really slept that long? My aunt quietly takes her place at the table with her now warm cup of coffee in hand. Picking up a breakfast taco, she unwraps it and starts eating, not saying a word. The silence is deafening and I'm not sure how much longer I can stand it.

"Why didn't you save my mom that night? Why me?"

Aunt Kat is not the type of person that is ever at a loss for words. The woman can effortlessly conjure up snarky retorts and witty comebacks, and is determined to have the last word in any conversation. But I've clearly hit the jackpot today, because aside from the choking noise that she makes as she tries to swallow, she doesn't say anything.

"So are we just going to pretend that this entire morning didn't happen? That I didn't see what I know I saw between you and Sam? That you didn't just see me frantically coming out of a nightmare?"

"I'm sorry. No, you're right, we do need to talk. I just don't know where to begin."

"Then start from the beginning. You said that I didn't need to do this alone, so I need answers. I need to understand how and why, and what we're doing here."

"The beginning. Okay. Well, I guess I'll start by telling you that you aren't human, at least that's not all you are."

A jumble of thoughts swirl in my mind, each one vying for attention as my aunt's revelation sinks in. Not human? How is that possible? My mom didn't have any powers. I would have know if she had. Wouldn't I? The question casts a shadow over my memories, and I start to sift through the fragmented moments of my childhood looking for anything that might seem odd. It's like trying to grasp at smoke, the memories slipping through my fingers as I struggle to piece together the puzzle. Aunt Kat's abilities, those small miracles she could conjure with a flick of her wrist, those were obvious signs that she was something else. Something magical. Flowers would be wilting in a vase one moment, and vibrant with life in another. Or she could wake up with eyeliner smeared down her face from not removing her makeup the night before, and with a wave of a hand be flawless. But all of that was after we jumped timelines, and after I already knew what she was. Did my mom do anything like that? Not that I can recall. My heart clenches as I confront the truth, that so much of my past remains obscured, a black void where memories of her should be. What about my dad? Again, I find myself trying to pull up the stories that John would tell me, but nothing that he told me about screams supernatural. Taking a deep breath and trying to remain calm, I press further.

"What do you mean? I need more words and a far better explanation than just saying that I'm not human."

My tone is flat, but it's the best that I can do. I don't have any powers, surely I would know if I did, and I'm starting to wonder if she has lost her mind. Aunt Kat takes a sip of her coffee before continuing, and I listen intently, hanging on to every word.

"Your mom was human, and I didn't know your dad, but I think it's only safe to assume that that's where your powers come from. You see, all paranormals have a special kind of energy. It's how others in our community know what you are, and frankly how strong you are. As a witch, we refer to that energy as our beacon. The stronger that your powers are, the more radiant your beacon is, and the further away that it can be felt. I know I've explained some of this to you before, but what I need to know before I go further is how much you remember from that night."

The weight of Aunt Kat's words settles heavily on my shoulders, and I can feel my hands trembling as I absorb the magnitude of what's been shared. I remember John once telling me that I have my dad's eyes. I was so young when he said it that I didn't grasp the concept of how you could have the same eyes as someone else. Never having the chance of meeting, or even seeing a picture of him, it's hard for me to match my imagination with reality. As I've gotten older and grasped an understanding of the phrase, every time I look in a mirror at my reflection a spark lights in my chest and I find myself holding on to the hope that what John said is the truth. That I do carry a piece of my dad with me. But now, the idea that I might carry a piece of him within me, something tangible linking us, has me reeling in excitement and anticipation. Since I didn't even know that I had powers, they must not be strong. The lack of information and new found knowledge of myself has me chomping at the bit to find out what they are. With a shaky voice, I share what I remember.

"I remember.... flashes mostly. I remember playing with my dolls just before answering the door for you. I think that you had gotten there early to help with decorations, and you had gone into the kitchen where mom was. I remember looking at the presents and being excited to open them when someone knocked at the door and I ran to open it. The rest is a blur, and I don't know how much comes from what really happened, or from the repetitive nightmares over the years.

In my nightmare, I dream that the door is kicked in and it throws me into the glass coffee table that we had in the living room. Men dressed in black come in the house shooting guns, and I can hear you screaming my name, and then everything goes dark. I don't remember anything else until the hotel room, and, well, you know the story from there."

Her hand is covering her mouth and she's nodding her head as I speak. I can see the wheels turning in her head. It's almost as if she's trying to decide just how much she should share, or how much I can handle.

"Whatever it is, just tell me. It can't be any worse than all of the things that I've imagined."

"Your mom and I didn't become friends on chance. When you were about six months old, I saw her pushing you in a stroller in the French Quarters down in New Orleans. I could sense your powers from a few blocks away, and felt called towards you. It's not uncommon for others in our community to be able to sense each other within the same city. It's not unusual for our kind to sense each other within the same city, but sensing someone before their sixteenth birthday, before their powers mature and become active, well, that's something rare. I walked the two blocks over to you, and as I got closer assumed they were coming from your mom. But once I was within a few feet from her, I knew without a doubt that it wasn't coming from her. The pull that I felt was coming from you. The stories I had heard of teenagers being able to be sensed early, usually meant that once their powers emerged they had additional abilities, like me. But never, had I ever, heard of a baby emitting such energy. I passed your mom in the street, not saying anything, and continued to watch from a distance. As time passed and I watched, I knew your mom wasn't one of us, but I never saw anyone in her life that explained you, and there was no indication that she knew what you were. That January, when you were nine months old, I bumped into your mom again at a local park. She didn't know who I was, or that I had been keeping tabs on you for the last three months, but we hit it off. We became the best of friends, and I knew one day you might need protecting. On your first birthday, my suspicions were confirmed when your beacon doubled in size. At the time our coven was in a disarray after the death of our leader and new leadership still finding their footing. I didn't know what to do, so I continued to do what I had been doing, staying close and keeping an eye on you."

How could I not know I have some type of power growing inside of me? Was her friendship with my mom ever even real, or was it all some sort of elaborate plan? Did she ever tell my mom? A weight of uncertainty overcomes me. I feel like the more information I am given, the less that I know. Lost in my thoughts, I nearly miss Aunt Kat's continuation.

"I asked your mom a few times about your dad, but she was never forthcoming with any information. The sadness in her eyes when she told me that he had passed in an accident before you were born told me that she had loved him. With each passing year, your beacon continued to grow exponentially, and it became abundantly clear that there was something different about you. Your beacon had some type of pull to it, like a weight drawing me in, making it harder and harder for me to stay away from you. I went from seeing you once a week or so, to nearly daily by the time your fourth birthday came around. I knew that if it was affecting me this way, that it might be doing the same to others nearby as well. My concerns were solidified when rumors began spreading through the southern coven of an unknown force pulling at them, some even speculating that it was an up and coming warlock. I knew it was only a matter of time before more eyes turned to you and until word got out to the other covens as well. What I didn't expect was it all to happen on your fifth birthday.

The way our beacon works, is that at the exact time of your birth, it shoots out a blast of energy before slowly waning away, like a ripple in the fabric of reality. When you're younger the blast is smaller, so it only takes about a day to go back down. As the year passes it will continue to gain power, reaching its maximum just before your next birthday when the next blast occurs. But the bigger the blast, the further it reaches, and the longer it takes for it to go back down. When the blast that night hit, it was felt through all of New Orleans and into some of the smaller surrounding towns. I don't know who those men were that broke in, but what I told you before was true, it was you that they were after.

When the new leadership of our coven took over, it took them a while to prove that they were worthy and could ensure our safety, and because of that there was some unrest within the coven. Some believed that a new head warlock was needed, and some wholeheartedly followed behind our current one. Your dream is accurate in what happened. I guess I was distracted and did not sense them coming before they were pounding on the door. But the moment that I did sense them, I ran towards the living room and that's when all hell broke loose. That scar on your forehead is not from a fall you took as a child, it's from being thrown into the glass table. When they began to fire off shots into the house, I was already closer to you than I was to your mom. If I had turned around to grab her before reaching you, I was in danger of being shot, and risked you being taken or dying at the mercy of their hands. I could see one of the men rushing towards you. I wasn't sure if you had sustained serious injuries from being hit by door, or from landing in the table, but I could see that you were bleeding everywhere and you had already begun to loose consciousness. So I grabbed you and skipped timelines to where we are now."

Dumbfounded, I sit patiently as Aunt Kat's words wash over me. Some of what she says resonates with me, matching what she told me in the beginning. Trying to maintain my composure, I begin mentally sorting through what is the truth and what I'm finding out to be lies. It's like standing on shifting ground, trying to grasp the reality of a world that has suddenly revealed its hidden layers. So much more makes sense as those missing puzzle pieces start to fall into place. Like when I had asked about the scar on my head, she told me I had fallen against the fireplace when running... that was a lie. Or when she told me that we were running because the men after us thought that I had seen something I wasn't supposed to. Yet for the life of me I couldn't remember what I had supposedly been witness to... only a partial lie, but still a lie.

"Were you telling the truth when you said that my mom died that night?"

"I saw her get shot just before we left, yes."

"And my dad, you really don't know who he was?"

"No"

"We don't travel on my birthday for fun, do we?"

"No. We travel because when that burst of energy comes from you, it's no longer felt just in our city, or limited to the surrounding cities. Hailey, your blast can be felt for hundreds of miles away. I never pick the same city twice, and I always pick large busy cities, so it's easier to hide ourselves."

The question that I really want to ask, but not sure I want to know the answer to is on the tip of my tongue. Closing my eyes, and bringing my coffee close to my lips, the question comes out as a whisper, so soft I almost can't hear it myself even though I'm the one who spoke it.

"Have you seen the men after me since that night?"

At first, I don't think she heard me, and I can hear the seconds tick by on the grandfather clock in the living room as I try to work up the nerve to ask it again. Taking a deep, fortifying sip of my tea, letting the warmth sooth my nerves, I sit up a little straighter in the chair. My palms moist against the porcelain cup, I steady myself to ask again, when I finally hear her answer. A single word, "Yes", has my heart racing, each beat a thunderous reminder of the danger I'm in. I struggle to catching my breath, each inhale coming in short, my lungs refusing to expand to their full capacity. There are no soothing thoughts or logical arguments that will make this brewing storm go away. I can't rationalize with myself, and instead find my mind going back to each of my birthdays. The memories of them play out like a blurry film reel, faces and interactions swirling together, and I fixate on each fleeting moment, hunting for any trace of the man with the tattoo. I turn my gaze inward, dissecting the actions and words of my aunt, questioning if I've overlooked any weird behavior. The memory slowly creeps its way back to me. A niggling feeling that I've encountered before, a hint of familiarity that dances at the edge of my consciousness. Frustration wells up within me as I grapple with it's elusiveness. Taking a deep breath, I shut my eyes in an attempt to shut out the world and delve deeper into my own mind. Just as I'm about to give in to the frustration and let go, the memory crashes into me with a force that steals my breath, an involuntary gasp escaping my lips.

"Last year. New York. On our last day there after we had taken the ferry back from Liberty Island, you insisted that we take the subway back to the hotel, even though it was only a few blocks away. I nearly fell down the subway stairs because you were running so fast even though I begged you to slow down. I tried to reason with you by saying we could just catch the next one, but you were on a mission and just increased your already fast pace. We were both out of breath and panting like we'd just ran a marathon when you pulled us through the doors just as they were closing. We laughed about it and you even made a joke about being out of shape and needing to hit the gym. It was then, wasn't it?"

The words slip out of my mouth, more a realization than a question, and by the look in her eyes, I know I'm right. The weight of that knowledge lands on me like a ton of bricks, leaving me stunned and speechless. How could I not have known? How did I not recognize the man that has haunted my dreams for the past decade? A shiver courses down my spine as a chilling thought takes root in my mind, gnawing at my thoughts like a persistent ache. What if i wasn't the man with the tattoo? What if the others who were there that night are still out there, lurking in the shadows, waiting for the right moment to resurface? What if was one of the them? I have been so fixated on the idea that all of them would come after me, that I never stopped to think they could be scattered, each one a separate threat, biding their time until they see fit to strike again

"Yes. I felt their presence in the city that morning, which is why we went to the Island. I thought it might be the safest place. It would guarantee that even if they could pinpoint your location, they would still have to ride the ferry to get to you, giving us ample time to catch a ferry back. I had no way of knowing that they would split up. I knew they were getting close, which lead me to believe that they had hopped a ferry and were headed towards the island. That's when I got us on the ferry that was disembarking back towards main land. But when we got off the boat, that feeling didn't go away. At first I didn't understand how that could be possible, but then it dawned on me that they must have split up. I wasn't sure if going underground would throw them off, but it was our best option. Just as we were starting to descend the stairs, I caught a glimpse of one of them heading towards us. That's when I rushed you to go faster."

Her words land like a heavy blow, and my worst fears manifest into reality. I close my eyes, attempting to conjure up any image of the other men from that night, but I can't. The faces, the features, they all blur together. Except for one distinct figure: the man with the tattoo. He's the only one etched into my mind with clarity, a haunting visage that has plagued my nightmares for years. Panic bubbles up within me as I grapple with the implications of not being able to picture the other men. How am I supposed to protect myself when I can't even identify who's after me?

"If I supposedly have such great powers, why can't I feel them? I clearly didn't feel them in New York. What am I even supposed to be feeling? Wait! Why can't I feel you?"

The words are coming out in a jumbled rush, the questions and my emotions colliding in a mess that I struggle to untangle. I feel like I have so many questions that I don't know where to start. Overwhelmed would be an understatement to the emotions that course through my veins. The extreme restlessness that has inched its way down every single nerve ending kicks up another notch the moment that I realize I can't put a finger on why I feel like this. Typically I know exactly what is causing my anxiety, and I can pinpoint the cause and fight the Monster back into captivity, releasing myself from its grip. But now, shrouded in half-truths and untold stories, I'm in unfamiliar territory.

"Magic seeks out other magic. You can't feel us because your powers have not evolved yet. For all intents and purposes, until your sixteenth birthday, you have no more power than our neighbors. But those of us whos magic is active, we can feel how strong you are."

I sit quietly giving myself time to digest all of the information I've just learned, and the food I've eaten. My coffee cup rests comfortably in my hands, its warmth having subsided from the initial pour and steam no longer rising, making it safer to sip without the threat of burning myself. A barrage of questions continue to flood my thoughts, but only two stand out in my mind. With a keen awareness of how delicate the balance of this conversation is, and a desire to avoid replicating the emotional upheaval of earlier, I start with what I think will be the easier question to answer.

"When did we come from?"

It's a simple question. One that doesn't need any additional context. I know it's 2016, but I have no idea what year it was before we arrived here in 2006, or even what year I was truly born.

"Hailey, I love that we have finally opened this door of communication, but we really need to leave soon if we are going to get out of here before you are officially fifteen. It's eleven o'clock, and we both still need to pack. It's going to take us at least an hour to get to the airport, find parking, shuttle over, and get checked in to our two twenty flight. Now that I think about it, we should probably pack carry-on bags since we aren't going to have time to check any bag in. I love you, but we're going to have to put a pin in this conversation."

As Aunt Kat rises from her seat, her gesture of affection, a gentle kiss atop my head, provides a fleeting sense of reassurance. Her footsteps recede as she heads toward her room, leaving me to navigate the thoughts swirling within me. Taking one last drink, emptying my cup, I stand up and place both of our cups in the dishwasher. Moving towards my room, I'm aware of the looming weight of unanswered questions, but she's right, we need to get going. Time away from this conversation will allow me to gather my thoughts and write down all of the questions and intrusive thoughts that are clouding my mind. Resolute in my decision, I retrieve my backpack from the hall closet, my fingers brushing over its familiar textures, I start a checklist of everything Google tells me that I'm going to need.

# 6

## Kat

The ride to the airport was anticlimactic with silence filling in the spaces between questions that revolved around our haphazardly packed bags and making sure that we did not forget anything. We both threw together our bags in a rush, only later to discover the oversight; she left behind her phone charger, and I managed to forget my swimsuit. Nothing that a stop by the local Walmart, once we land, will not fix. To streamline our transition at the airport, I've made arrangements with a local shuttle service, The Parking Spot. Pulling into its gravel driveway, I am able to scan my reservation on my phone at the electronic booth. It only takes a second for the kiosk to whir to life and print out my receipt, allowing me to drive straight to the corresponding parking space that is located at the top of the ticket. As if the universe knows that we need time on our side, a bright yellow and black bus pulls up next to us as we are grabbing our backpacks from the car. A slight wave of relief rushes over me knowing that we do not have to waste time waiting for a bus. The engine's hum interlaces with the surroundings. While we wait for it to come to a stop and open its doors, I start a mental list of the questions that I anticipate Hailey will ask. With each query, I fashion a thoughtful response in advance, considering the ones that will yield straightforward answers, and the topics that require more careful handling. There are some things that she just cannot know yet, and I need to decide how I am going to handle that.

Stepping onto the bus, we manage to snag the last available seats, positioned adjacent to each other. Because we were the last two to board making the bus full, the driver is able to skip the others waiting in line and head directly towards our designated terminal. Our backpacks find a temporary home on our laps, and as the engine roars to life, we brace ourselves for the inevitable jolts and judders during our ride.

The drive doesn't take more than ten minutes, and I look at my phone as we disembark the bus. It is almost one thirty, and because we are not checking bags we might have some time to kill. Stepping through the sliding glass doors, I steer us toward the self-check-in stations that line the left side of the terminal navigate through its digital prompts, swiftly printing the boarding passes that were secured during the chaotic moments of packing. Typically one of the downfalls to purchasing tickets so close to departure is that it is not guaranteed that we will sit together, but today it is my saving grace. My eyes scan the printed details, and the tension that I did not realize I was hold in my shoulders wanes. I'll be occupying seat 14C, while Hailey's spot is reserved at 22A. Putting on my best upset face, I break the news.

"Sorry kiddo, it looks like we will not be sitting together this flight."

"That's okay. Maybe on the way back."

I can see the disappointment in her eyes, but I am grateful that she doesn't press or suggest that we see if someone wants to do a seat swap once we board.

I know waiting in line for TSA is half the battle when you are racing against the clock. Fortunately for me, forty-five minutes of our time is eaten up in line as we slowly snake our way forward towards security. Preparing ourselves to go through the metal detector has Hailey distracted, conveniently preventing her from peppering me with questions during the wait. With no time to spare, we power walk as fast as possible to our gate. Just as we are approaching, I hear the announcement for priority boarding, catering to families and those with young children. Yet again I am relieved at my luck. The more time that I have to formulate my answers, the better off we will be. I shoot Sam a text letting him know we made it and will be boarding soon, and immediately get a response back.

"In the swamp lmk if u need me."

It is short and to the point, just like Sam usually is. He told me last week that he would need to go to Louisiana soon to settle some disputes, but I had not realized that it would be this weekend. Giving him a thumbs up response, I quickly ensure that the Netflix shows I downloaded have finished before putting my phone on airplane mode before slipping it into my hoodie pocket.

The flight itself is uneventful, marked by minimal turbulence, and we land a few minutes before five thirty. Not wanting to take a risk on waiting for an Uber and be late getting into the city, we make a beeline for the car rental counter, opting for whatever they can offer. By the time six o'clock rolls around we are cruising down highway 836 in a brand new vibrant red Mazda headed west. From the corner of my eye, I observe Hailey pull a piece of paper from the front pocket of her jeans. I watch as she studies it with intent before laying it across her thigh as she grabs a pen from her backpack and begins to write. Amusement creeps across my face as I chuckle inwardly when her face contorts into her characteristic "focus face" mode, tongue slightly protruding from the corner of her mouth, while she pours effort into her writing.

"What's that?"

"Thoughts and questions."

"For me?"

I already know the answer, and the quick "Yep" that I hear next only solidifies my suspicion. I am thankful that I took time on the plane to begin to prepare myself for our next conversation. Trying to anticipate what questions she would ask and how I would answer, knowing that I could not possibly guess everything that she would ask, all the while trying to give myself a solid foundation to start with. She has clearly taken the time to do the same seeing that the page is written on front and back.

As we pull up to a red light, just before turning into our hotel, I feel the warm blast of air hit me so hard I can't help but to lean away from it and push myself into the door.

Without needing to glance at the clock, I already know that it's 6:06. Closing my eyes, I send out my feelers. I have already done this once today when I got off the plane. While I was waiting for Hailey to disembark from plane and walk out of the jetway, I tried to establish a baseline understanding of the city's energy and the people present. Admittedly, it's not foolproof; not everyone's energy can be detected from afar. However, it's not the people who were here when we landed that I'm concerned about. My primary concern lies with the four energy signatures on the outskirts of my perception, individuals who weren't there just thirty minutes ago.

The light switches to green, and I guide the car into the Meridian hotel's premises. After parking, I pull out my phone to text Sam that we arrived safety and the impending unwelcome guests, but instead am met with a text from him, a message I need to read twice to truly grasp. Reminding myself that we'd anticipated this scenario and had prepared accordingly, I breathe a sigh of readiness. Last year, based on coven reports, we deduced that Hailey's energy surge was felt across approximately twelve hundred miles. This information significantly contributed to our decision to remain within the southern coven's protection this year. After reading Sam's text once more and composing a reply, I slide my phone back into my backpack's side pocket and exit the car. As we round the front of the Mazda and start walking towards the hotel, I let Hailey know that Sam is on his way. I can see the gears turning in her head as her expression twists into a look of perplexed shock. Before she can utter a word of rebuttal, I throw up my hand in a stop motion and let her know I will explain once we're inside the security of our room.

Walking into the lobby, I am immediately struck by the blend of modern and boho aesthetics gracing every inch of the hotel. Hanging round wire baskets host suspended plants from the ceiling, and the front desk boasts an inventive assembly of antique suitcases. The wraparound shelving behind the desk is a treasure trove of curiosities, and to our left sleek black stairs beckon us toward the upper floors. After checking in, we are instructed to the second floor where our room awaits. Upon entering, we're met with sandstone colored tile floors and pristine white duvets adorning our queen sized beds. Walking further into the room, I pull aside the sheer curtains, revealing a pleasant surprise, a balcony offering a mesmerizing view of the pool and the swaying palm trees beyond. Sitting my backpack on the closest bed, I approach the sliding glass doors, finding solace in its view. However, my serenity is short lived, ended by the dreaded question that I knew was coming, yet don't want to answer.

"Why is Sam coming here?"

I can answer this a few different ways, and I weigh my options. I can lie and tell her that he is just wanting to spend her birthday with us. Sam has been a steady fixture in her life since we arrived in Houston, so it's a believable lie. I could also tell her the complete truth, but in doing that I would also have some explaining to do to Sam as well. Neither of those options are really viable, so as usual, I opt for something in the middle. Not the complete truth but not a blatant lie.

"Sam was in Louisiana when your burst of energy released. Hailey, he felt it all the way there. That's over eight-hundred miles away from us! He knows that there are people after you and what is at stake.Sso he wants to be here to help keep you safe. Also, I need to let you in on another little secret." The look on Hailey's face has me questioning if she can take any more surprises. I debate for only a second before deciding that this will likely be the pivotal moment that will determine the trajectory of our conversation. "Sam is a warlock. I guess I should have started with that."

Short, simple, and to the point. I can tell by her reaction, or lack thereof, that the information I have given her has her in a mental maze as she tries to find her way out. I have tried to be strategic and allow her to ask the questions she wants, all the while trying to stay one step ahead, guiding her in the direction of my liking. If she gets too close to the truth before its time, I run the risk of everything crumbling down around me. All of the work I have put into keeping her safe will have been for nothing.I watch as her mouth opens, closes, and then opens again as she decides what part of that announcement she wants to tackle first. Just like I hoped, she takes the bait.

"That's what the looks between y'all have been, isn't it? I wasn't imagining things! How long has he known that I have these so-called powers? At least six months, right?"

"Sam has known all along. It was not a coincidence that we moved next door to him. I told you when we first moved here that we had to meet him because he owned the house that we would be renting, but that was only partially true. Sam is the leader of our coven, and he is an extremely powerful warlock. He has known from the day he met you that you were something else, something extraordinary. When he felt how strong you were, he insisted that we live next door so that he can keep an eye on things. But to answer your question, yes, that is what the looks have been between us. Because he is stronger than me, his reach is further than mine and he has been able to estimate how far away from home you need to be to keep Houston a safe haven for us. It's like a radar of sorts. If your power reaches a one-hundred-mile radius, you can also feel anyone within that parameter. If they are outside of that radius, you would not know they existed unless they got closer. The weaker their powers, the smaller the blip on your radar, and if their powers are strong than yours, they will encompass your entire radar. The exception to this is someone like Sam, who has powers so strong the entire coven can feel him regardless of how far their power reaches. Sweetheart, you are also an exception to this rule. This year, Sam estimated your blast would be felt for more than fifteen hundred miles, so he insisted that our best option would be for us to stay in the safety of our own coven."

I watch as Hailey digests all of this information, and I begin to think I have underestimated how much she has previously pieced together. She doesn't seem too shocked by this information, after all none of this has sent her into a full blown panic attach that I was fully prepared for. Instead of jumping into a plethora of questions that were spurred by this new information, she pulls out a piece of paper that she had crumpled in her front pocket. Recognizing it immediately as the one she had in the car, I lean in closer for a better view. What catches my eye is not the number of questions she has thought of, instead it is the variety of colors that are written on the piece of paper. There are questions in blue, black, red, and even purple ink. With an even closer examination, a smile crosses my face and I let out a faint laugh as I realize she has color coded her questions in what I assume as red being the most important, black being less important, and purple being her favorite.

"Two questions. You get two questions Hailey, and then we are headed to the pool to relax and enjoy the view. I think we both need to unwind, and can use a mental break. We can go over some more once Sam arrives."

"Oh. Um, okay-hold on."

While she stands reading over her list debating on which are the most two important questions to ask, I take a moment to admire how much she looks like her mom. No longer a cotton top, as she has aged, her blonde hair has darkened into the same sandy brown that Sarah's was with subtle hints of natural highlights. Her curls, no longer small ringlets, instead they are now a steady flow of waves from the weight of her long, thick hair. From her profile view, I can see the way her nose tips up at the end before following it down to her full lips. The same lips I can remember telling Sarah that people would pay thousands of dollars for. Her small narrow chin and sharp jawline stand out against her otherwise soft details. But her eyes, those she didn't get from her mom. No, those came from her dad.

"Okay, I think I've got them. First one, why does this happen only on my birthday?"

"Hailey, when we jumped timelines, it created a small hole in the space time continuum. That hole is repaired once you go back to the time you came from. But because we never went back, it's left what we call a barrier. Each year, when your burst of energy gives out that pulse, it opens the barrier back up allowing the men to travel through it, and stays open until the power radiating from you shrinks again. Think of it like a boat towing a person who's skiing. The boat, meaning you, is driving forward while leaving a wake, meaning your power, behind it. When the boat turns off, it can still coast forward, but the wake that was behind it dissipates, and the person skiing can no longer stay on top of the water. We don't believe any of the men after you possess chronokinesis, and therefor they rely on your power to keep them here. Once your power is no longer radiating in excess, they have to go back to where they came from before the barrier closes."

"Do I get to ask questions about my questions? Or do I literally only get two questions?"

"Two questions Hailey, I will answer additional questions later when Sam is here, so that he can help me field them."

"Ugh! Okay, fine. Do you know if the men are here, in Miami?"

"They are not here yet. But they are within two hundred miles, because I can feel them. So it's safe to assume that they will be here by morning. Now, how about you go ahead and change into your swim suit? I'll walk over to Target to grab me one and maybe some snacks, and meet you down by the pool. Sam will be here in a few hours, and we can talk more then."

The disappointed look in Hailey's eyes almost has me feeling bad for stopping her line of questions. I know that she has more, and that she deserves answers, but I truly do feel like it would be best if Sam were here before we go further. Without a second look, I grab my hotel key and wallet, and walk out the door.

Target is less than a quarter of a mile from the hotel, and it takes me less than five minutes to get there. Walking in, I immediately run into where the swimwear is located, and see a purple bikini that screams Hailey. Even though she brought one, I go ahead and add it into my cart so that she can have one to wear when the other is wet and grab myself two as well. After grabbing Oreo's, M&M's, Pop-Tarts, and some other junk food, I quickly check out through a self checkout lane and head back to the hotel. I know that Hailey isn't in any immediate danger because I can sense the men are still pretty far away, but I don't want to leave her out of my sight any longer than I have to.

Bypassing the check in station and heading straight upstairs to our room. Grabbing my swimsuit out of the Target bag as I enter our hotel room, I drop the bags on the bed. I change into the red one piece that I bought for myself and after searching through my backpack I locate the black cover up that I remembered to pack. Grabbing the room key I head downstairs to find Hailey floating on her back in the pool. Signaling to her that I'm back, I get a small wave in return and let her know that I am going to be sitting at the bar if she needs anything. Getting a thumbs up reply, and an acknowledgment that she doesn't want a tea or soda, I head towards the bar. Picking a seat at the bar with a full view of the pool, I order a Sea Breeze with an extra shot of vodka, and watch in amusement as Hailey attempts to do a handstand under the water. Fixated on watching Hailey, I am startled when the bar tender sits my drink in front of me a few minutes later. Without pause, I take a long gulp before sitting it back down on the bar and try to relax while we wait for Sam's arrival.

# 7

# Hailey

I've lost track of time when the sudden cry of 'CANNONBALL' echoes across the pool. Before I can move to see who yelled it, a tidal wave crashes into me from behind, its forceful splash engulfing my head. Water drips down my face as I quickly push my hair away, turning to find Sam emerging from the ripples that he created.

"You made it!"

I yell as loud as I can. We aren't that far apart, but the hotel bar is only a few feet away and has a night life of its own, with music pumping and crowds gathering. Shaking his head like a dog his sopping hair flings droplets in a watery arc, and a wide grin forms on his face as he starts wading my way. When Aunt Kat told me that he would be coming out here, I couldn't understand why. But once she explained what he is, I understood. If I'm being honest, it's comforting for me to have him here. Sam has a calming presence about him, and no matter what is going on, he's able to make me feel better without ever saying a word.

"I sure did. Are you hungry yet? Kat said y'all haven't eaten since getting here... and no, the Oreo's and Pop-Tarts that she bought at Target don't count as food."

"I'm starving. I could literally eat my own arm at this point. But Aunt Kat said she wanted to wait on you in case you hadn't eaten either."

"She's right, I haven't. Let's get out and order some of that pizza you talked about this morning."

Heading towards the stairs to exit the pool, I can feel Aunt Kat's gaze following our every move. I spot her immediately still sitting in the same spot at the bar that she's been in since getting back from Target. Aside from bringing me the occasional cup of Dr. Pepper, she hasn't moved, but is now watching us intently. Going up the stairs that lead out of the pool we grab our towels off of the closest lounge chair and make a beeline for her. We take our seats on adjacent bar stools, and Sam raises an eyebrow playfully, seemingly unfazed by the water dripping from our suits onto the tiled floor.

"What kind of pizza do you girls like?"

Excitement courses through me as I hastily wrap my towel around me. I rush to make sure that I'm the first to give Sam an answer. Ordering pizza has always been an argument in our house, with me loving Hawaiian and Aunt Kat loves supreme. How she eats anything with black olives on it is beyond me. More often than not we settle the debate with a game of rock-paper-scissors. Now that Sam is here, he can break the tie.

"Hawaiian!"

"Supreme!"

Both Aunt Kat and I answering at the same time with different answers has Sam looking back and forth between the two of us like we have multiple heads. He clearly doesn't know the war he just started.

"So half Hawaiian and half supreme?"

"Then what are you going to eat, Sam?"

Aunt Kat's quick and sassy reply has me laughing out loud, but she's right. We can both put away a half of a pizza by ourselves, so we're going to need more than one box for the three of us.

"Alright then, one Hawaiian, and one supreme it is."

Walking towards the stairs in the lobby, I hear Sam tell Aunt Kat that his room is on the third floor, and that he'll meet us back in ours once he's changed. When Aunt Kat and I arrive on our floor, I call dibs on the shower and rush towards the door before she can beat me to it. Playing along, she races after me, but the element of surprise is on my side. I reach the door just moments before her and snatch the key card out of her hand as she playfully pushes me to the side trying to get in before me. Giving my best Emmy winner speech when the light on the lock turns green I head straight to the bathroom to begin warming up the shower the moment we enter our room.

Taking my sweet time I relish the warmth of the water in contrast to the cold air blowing from the A/C in the room. By the time that I finish showering, get dressed, and walk back out into the room, Sam and my aunt are sitting on the balcony talking. The smell of pizza invades my senses causing my mouth to involuntarily salivate in anticipation. Eager to join the conversation, I grab a paper plate and two slices before heading out to the balcony to sit with them. As I put the first piece in my mouth, my taste buds are immediately overcome by the vibrant sweetness and tropical flavor of the pineapples. Lost in the delightful taste, I momentarily tune out the conversation around me. Sam is mid sentence when my brain finally catches up to my ears.

"Who's going to be here tonight?"

The answer is already in the back of my head and I can feel it in my gut, but I need to hear the answer out loud.

"I was saying that the men are close, and will likely be in Miami by tonight."

The weight of Sam's words hits me like a physical blow to the chest, the impact reverberating through my entire being. Despite anticipating his response, there is no amount of preparation that could have prepared me for the way it would make me feel. My heart pounds with such intensity that it sends aching pulses through my chest, and an unwelcome chill has begun to creep its way up my spine causing goosebumps to prick across every inch of my flesh. This has never happened before. With the exception of last year, if what my aunt told me is true, we've never been close to being caught. Even last year they didn't show up until our last day in New York. The proximity of their presence now raises a multitude of questions, each one vying for attention in my overwhelmed mind. Why are they so close already? Better yet, *how* are they so close already? What does this mean for us? Admid the chaotic swirl of questions flying around inside my head, I don't know where to start. So, instead of trying to organize and prioritize them, I blurt out the first one that my brain can form into a coherent sentence.

"How are we going to keep them away from us if they are already so close? Last year we only had to stay hidden for one day, the last day, and we barley managed that! How are we going to do it for multiple days? Also, how long do we actually need to be here? Why can't we just get on a plane and go somewhere else?"

"Your Aunt and I were talking about that while you were in the shower and I think we have a plan. But to answer your question about the plane, we have reason to believe at least one of the men after you has the ability to teleport. We believe he can only teleport a small distance at a time, but because your power is so strong this year, it means they will be able to follow you no matter where you go. I believe Kat told you about me... about what I am, correct?"

Nodding my head, I hang on to every word that Sam is saying while I recall what Aunt Kat had told me about him. Leader of her coven, warlock, super powerful, I got it... I think?

"Okay, good, then I don't have to catch you up to speed on that. I can go ahead and jump right to the plan that your aunt and I have come up with. Right now, we are banking on their powers being less than mine or yours. Now keep in mind that this theory has never been tested. Normally we all stay within our own territories, so it is difficulty for anyone to know how strong someone else is outside of their coven. Unless of course that, that person was to travel, and even then it may be hard to tell how strong their powers are. Aside from the warlocks who lead each coven, no one's powers have ever been close to matching ours until you came along. The idea is that they won't be able to differentiate between my powers and yours if we stay close together. They should be able to tell that someone powerful is near, but because each of our powers surpass their reach, we are hoping that they won't know there is more than one person responsible for what they are feeling. Actually I'm not sure that I'm describing this correctly or making much sense."

Sam gets up and walks inside to the dresser that sits against the wall in front of the beds, and grabs the small note pad and pen that the hotel leaves for you to write notes on before walking back out to the balcony and sitting down. Engrossed in thought, he concentrates on the notepad for a minute or two, before sketching what appears to be three circles. Almost immediately after drawing them he scratches them out and flips to the next page. Pausing for a moment before drawing anything else, he looks up and asks if either me or Aunt Kat have different colored pens. Walking inside, I head straight for my backpack and grab the satchel of pens I used earlier for the notes I was making on the plane. then head back outside. Returning to the balcony, I hand the satchel to Sam, positioning myself just behind his left shoulder to get a clear view of his drawings. In black ink, he meticulously draws four circles, arranging them in a two by two pattern, each touching the others to form a box. He then grabs a green pen out of the satchel and draws another circle that surrounds the first four. Putting the green pen back, he grabs the purple pen and draws another circle just outside of the green one. Turning around to face me, he takes a deep breath, makes eye contact and starts to explain.

"The four black circles represent the men after you and their powers. Keep in mind what I said earlier, we aren't sure how strong these men's powers are individually or as a group. However, we have reason to believe at least one of them has additional tricks up his sleeve, so his power source might be larger than the other three. The green circle represents me and my powers, which leaves the purple to represent you."

He stops for a moment before moving on. Although I can't take my eyes off of the drawing, I can feel him staring at me, gauging my response to finding out that my powers are apparently stronger than his. Determined to keep my face flat and not surrender to the internal battle of *OMG* and *WTF*, all while trying to remember how to breathe. I ask the only question that my brain can process at the moment.

"Where is Aunt Kat in all of this?"

I can tell that I've caught him by surprise when his eyebrows shoot all the way up to his hairline and he opens his mouth, letting it hang there for a moment before responding.

"Good question. We're not exactly sure where she falls on this map. Her powers in relation to the men are unknown at this time. She might have stronger powers than all of the men, or she could be stronger than one or two while being equal to the others. I didn't include her because of that unknown factor. But as you can see, both my powers and yours, hopefully, overlap each of the men's powers. If we are correct with this theory, and in order for the plan to work, we have to keep you hidden with me in public view. Best case scenario, if the men come anywhere close to us, they will see me and just assume that the power is solely coming from me and leave."

"And worst case scenario?"

"To be honest Hailey, we don't have a plan for that. This is new territory for all of us, so we're kind of flying by the seat of our pants."

I guess a half baked plan is better than no plan at all, so I roll with it. Sam and Aunt Kat continue to talk and I try to follow their conversation and plans being made, but their voices have become a far away echo. With an overwhelming amount of new information to digest, I've lost my appetite and I'm too exhausted to stay and entertain their conversation.

"If it's okay with y'all, I'm going to head to bed. From the sound of it, we really don't know what the next few hours are going to look like, much less the next few days, so I'd like to get some sleep while I can."

"Of course, Sweetie. Today has been a long day for all of us, especially you. Sam and I can go back to his room and finish our conversation so we don't keep you awake."

I smile softly and offer my gratitude. As we all walk into the chilly room, I lay down in the bed closest to the balcony and wave my goodbyes as they walk out of the main door. Aunt Kat is right, today has been a long day for me, physically, mentally and especially emotionally. As I try to relax I find myself tossing and turning as I mull over all of the information that I've learned in the last few hours. Sleep doesn't find me easy, but when it does it captures me by a choke hold, throwing me back into my past.

***

*My vision is coming back in the same type of tunnel that it left me, only gaining light rather than drowning in darkness. I can hear a voice break through the deafening sound of my heart beating in my head, recognizing it as Aunt Kat's. I try to follow it as my vision continues to clear. Immediately I realize that I'm laying down, and I spot Aunt Kat sitting on the floor just to the left of my head, tears streaking her face as she runs her hands through my hair.*

*"Hailey, can you hear me?"*

*Nodding my head yes, I move to sit up and grab my head as I moan out in pain. The dull ache of my head from earlier has now amplified and is coupled with a pounding throb that matches the beat of my heart. Sitting up is out of the question, so instead I do a worm-like crawl over to my aunts lap and lay my head there. Closing my eyes hoping that my head will stop hurting, I listen to the comforting sound of her shushing*

*"You gave me quite the scare Sweet Girl, are you okay?"*

*"My head hurts. I thought you were a bad guy trying to get me. What happened? Where are we? Where's my mom?"*

*Something doesn't feel right. The memories of waking up in this hotel room come back to me, bombarding all of my emotions. Tears threaten to spill from my eyes as I say the words that are echoing in my head. I don't know what's wrong, but I know that I'm hurt, I'm not where I last remember being, and my mom isn't here with us.*

*"Hailey, what is the last thing that you remember?"*

*"I remember looking at my birthday presents by the fire place."*

*"You don't remember anything else?"*

*The tone of her voice has the tears that were once threatening to spill out, now trailing down my cheeks. What am I supposed to remember? I know something bad happened, I can tell by the sadness in her eyes.*

*"Where is my mommy?"*

*"I'm so sorry sweet girl."*

*Trying to hold back her tears, Aunt Kat chokes on her words before telling me that some bad men had broken into our house with guns and that she was only able to save me. I don't understand what she means until she leaves no room for interpretation.*

*"Your Mommy is in heaven now."*

*Burying my face further into my aunts lap, I cry until there are no tears left. Getting us off of the floor, my aunt picks me up and carries me to the bed, singing softly, and holding me until I stop shaking. Reaching up, I absentmindedly rub the bandage on my forehead and instantly am reminded of the cuts all over me.*

*"What happened to me? How did Mommy go to heaven? How did we get to a hotel?"*

*I have more questions than answers, but the anguish in Aunt Kat's face has me stopping with those three. Wiping her cheeks before resuming to run her hand through my hair she tells me a tale that I have absolutely no memory of.*

*"You heard someone knock on the door, and when you went to open it, some bad men broke into the house. They hurt your mommy, and when you went to run away you hit your head on the fire place. Everything happened so fast, I'm not sure how you got the rest of the scratches. Your mommy was worried that this might happen, she said that the two of you might have seen these bad men do something you weren't supposed to see. She knew I had special powers, so she asked me to keep you safe if they ever showed up. When they broke down the front door, your mommy was hurt, so I ran to you and brought you here."*

*"What did I see them do? What kind of special powers do you have? Do you have special powers like Cinderella's Godmother?"*

*"I don't know what you and your mommy saw, I never asked. But kind of like Cinderella's Godmother, or maybe even like Tinker-bell. I have a little bit of magic in me just like them."*

*I smile a little before a big yawn escapes me unexpectedly as I try to ask more questions.*

*"Do you think I will ever see my Mommy again?"*

*"I don't know Sweetheart. I hope so. Lets get you out of that dress and try to get some sleep. We can talk some more when you wake up."*

*I try to fight it, but yawning again I can feel sleep creeping up on me faster than my talking can counter it. I watch as my aunt walks over to the corner by the door and pulls a pajama set from a Walmart bag that was sitting on the floor. After she unties the bow in the back of my dress, I raise my arms up so that she can help me change. Aunt Kat tosses my old dress into the same corner that she retrieved my pajamas from, before helping me into the new ones and laying back down. Just as I'm drifting off, I feel Aunt Kat slide further down in bed and cuddle into me, allowing sleep to claim her too.*

# 8

# Sam

From the day that I met Kat and Hailey, Kat has never been fully transparent with me. Most times I let it slide, but with what's at stake right now, I need the whole truth.

"What all does Hailey know? I need you to be completely honest with me here Kat. No shady shit, and no lies."

"She knows about you Sam. She knows that you are the leader of our coven, and are an incredibly strong warlock. She knows that it is not a coincidence that we moved next door to you, and you just broke the news on how strong her powers are. She knows her mom was human, and that we don't know exactly what or who her dad was, but assume that his genes were passed down to her, resulting in her powers. She knows that we jumped timelines in order to keep her safe, and that her mom died that night. She also knows that the men are after her because of her powers. I have not answered all of her question, because I thought it would be easier if you were here to field some of them, but she knows enough."

"Does she know when y'all came from?"

"No, and just like you, she is not going to. I do not think that it will benefit her at all at this point. We still don't know what powers she's going to have when she turns sixteen, or what havoc she'll create if it's possible for her to get to a timeline in an attempt to save her mom."

I really hate when Kat makes fair points in an argument. If there is one thing to count on when it comes to her, she is consistently level-headed and witty. I can always guarantee that she will be ten steps ahead of where I think she is, armed with a comeback for anyone who dares to get in her way. As usual, she's right. Teens are unpredictable with their magic when it comes to fruition, and there's no reason to believe that Hailey will be any different. If she's able to manipulate time like her aunt, or distort the present, there is a good chance that she will try to go back and save her mom or dad. There is a delicate manner in which those powers can be used, and manipulation like that is not something that should be played with. I also understand why Kat won't tell me either. She's risked so much for Hailey, that she can't risk being betrayed. All it would take is one single person in this time, who also possesses chronokinesis, to find out and track down the men after them, and bring them here using their power. The best kept secrets are the ones that aren't shared, so I let her keep it.

Closing my eyes, I put my feelers out. Kat does the same, and I know that she feels exactly what I do. The men are getting closer, making a beeline straight for Miami. Saying a silent prayer, I pray that our plan works out. If we can make it through this weekend, we will be in the clear for one more year. Hailey's power will shrink back down, forcing the men to go back to their original place in time. By the next time the barrier opens back up, Hailey will possess her powers and be able to protect herself from whatever, or whoever is after her. Wondering if I should call in reinforcements, I decide to hold off. Grabbing my phone of the night stand where I left it charging, I shoot my Second in Command, J, a quick text. 'Made it here. All good for now. Update soon.' Hitting send, I lay it back down just as it buzzes again letting me know that he replied, 'K just lmk. I'll be down in The Big Easy if you need me'. The text has me laughing as I turn back around to face Kat.

"What is so funny?"

"Nothing, just my Second always chomping at the bit to get in on some action."

Kat's quizzical expression only has me laughing more. She's never met any of the other leaders, and I make a mental note to introduce them the next time he's in town. Most of the covens warlocks have their Second in Command either live with them, or close by, in the event that anything ever goes down, they have immediate back up. High-powered wizards located in the larger cities across each of the states the coven covers help with day-to-day operations. However, that's not how I run mine. J was happily married and living a life down in New Orleans when I stepped into the Warlock role and was chosen to lead our coven. I couldn't bare causing an upheaval in his life. especially now that him and his wife will be expecting early next year. It is completely out of the question.

Instead, I run the headquarters out of Houston, and travel frequently between there, New Orleans, and all of our other cities that make up the Southern Coven. I find that being present makes for stronger leadership, with fewer issues, and my style is what separates me from the warlocks who lead the other three major covens.

"Do you think they will be able to identify us as soon as they get here?"

My knee jerk reaction is to say 'probably'. They've been chasing Kat and Hailey for a decade, and last year they got a good feel for Hailey's power. I'm confident that if it were just Kat and her, that the men would be able to isolate them immediately. The fact that they made a beeline straight for Miami once the barrier opened verifies my concerns and also has me feeling uneasy.

"Honestly, Kat, I'm really banking on my powers to throw them for a loop. If this doesn't work, I'm afraid I don't know how we are going to keep her safe."

My words come out in an exasperated tone, making me realize just how worried I am. This moment is something that we both knew might happen, but prayed would never come. I can see the fire in Kat's eyes though, and I know without a doubt that she won't go down without a fight and that these men will only get to Hailey over her dead body.

"I can call in reinforcements as an absolute last resort, but if I do that, I can't promise you that y'all's secret won't get out."

Compromising them is the last thing that I want to do, as I find myself mentally trying to tally up who I can trust to help. My Second in Command is a no-brainer, and David from Georgia is a good contender.

"Let's keep that in the back of our mind, as you said, and initiate it as an absolute last resort. If we truly need the help, I am sure being compromised will be the last of our worries."

She's right, if we need to bring in others, it's because we've exhausted all other efforts at keeping them safe. If you would have told me eight years ago that I would be here today, I would have laughed at you. I was living my best life. At that time, I was living my best life, blissfully unaware that a child and her aunt would show up in my town a year later and in an instant of meeting them, turn my world upside down. The day that I met Hailey, I knew that she was special. In all my years as a wizard, and the decades after my rise to being the Southern Coven's head warlock, have I ever encountered someone quite like her. Kat told me the night that we met that she knew Hailey's mom was a human, but I have my suspicions about that. Hailey's dad being an unknown supernatural doesn't entirely explain the remarkable strength of Hailey's powers. As witches and wizards, we can detect others that carry the same magic as us, such as the Faye, but if Hailey's mom belonged to a different supernatural group, Kat would have never felt it. In the seven years since Kat and Hailey came into my life, I've grown to love them like family. Regardless of the secrets that they choose to keep, or unknowingly have, I will lay down my life for them.

"Tell me about Hailey's mom."

"There's not much to tell Sam. She was an amazing mother to Hailey, and a dear friend to me. She was the type of person that you wanted to have in your corner. She fought hard, and loved even harder. She was cheated out of life way too soon."

"Are you sure she wasn't some type of supernatural?"

Kat's laugh is deep and hearty, coming out in a short spurt with a sarcastic undertone. I'm sure she thinks I've lost my mind, since she's told me from the get-go that Hailey's mom was nothing but a mere human, yet things just don't add up. One look at my face tells her that I'm serious, and has her eyes going wide.

"Are you kidding me right now Sam? No she was not, I would have known! I spent five years spending more days than not with them. I would not have missed something like that. Nothing that she did, and no one that she hung out with ever gave me any indication that they were anything but human. Don't you think that if she could have, she would have saved herself and her daughter? We would not be here right now if she had any sort of power in her."

"I get it, I do. But something isn't adding up here Kat. Tell me how some kid can have powers that are stronger than any of the coven warlocks? We've never seen anything like this. Her mom wasn't a witch or Faye, I get that, but what if she had some type of magic that isn't from the same origin as ours? Her dad must have been a wizard, and that's were she gets some of her power from, but that doesn't account for how strong she is. Have you noticed that the aura of her beacon is gold? I've never seen anything like it in my life."

"I'm telling you now Sam, Hailey's mom did not have anything special like that about her. I don't know where Hailey gets her power, or why she seems to be an anomaly, but you suggesting that her mother had some hidden powers is the same as you saying that she could have done something to save herself, or her daughter that night. That's bullshit and you know it Sam. She did not choose to leave us or die that night. They took her from us, and there was nothing that I could do to save her. So don't you come at me and tell me that she could have saved herself, but chose not to."

"Look, I didn't mean to upset you. I know that she was your best friend. I'll stop asking, but promise me that you will think about it too, okay? There has to be something that explains Hailey;s powers, and maybe we're both missing it, but I think that we can both agree that something is going on."

I must have really pissed her off, because Kat gets up and walks out of my room without uttering another word. It's not the way I envisioned concluding our conversation or the day in general, but it is what it is. Hopefully by morning she will have cooled down and allowed logic to prevail. I've racked my brain throughout the years, and haven't been able to come up with anything that makes sense. I have exasperated all avenues to the point I have just written it off as a freak occurrence, expecting her power to eventually stop growing. But this year when her power surpassed mine, I knew that the little voice in the back of my head all these years was right, I just wish that it had answers to go along with all of its questions. Picking up my phone, I send a message to J letting him know to be packed and ready to go if we need him, then make my way towards the shower.

Running a towel through my hair as I walk out of the bathroom, I hear my phone buzz. I'm surprised that J is still awake at this hour. Moving the white comforter back, I slide in between the sheets and settle myself before reaching over and grabbing my phone to see what he said. To my surprise, it's not him though, and instead I find myself smiling like a teenaged boy who just got told the hottest girl in school likes him. Sending a quick reply I roll over and close my eyes to get some sleep in anticipation of tomorrows events. However, all I can think about is that text.

'*Sorry our weekend got cut short, guess you'll have to wait to see what that surprise was when you get back. Be safe in Miami, I can't wait to be back in your arms.*'

# 9

# Kat

Stretching, I roll over in bed only for my eyes to be assaulted by the rays of sunlight shining through the sheer curtains that hang from the sliding glass door leading to the balcony. The clock on the bedside table indicates that it's after ten in the morning. As I glance over at the other bed, looking past the clock, I can see Hailey is still sound asleep. Deciding to get up, I roll out of bed, I grab a flowing maxi dress out of my backpack, along with my sandals from the floor near the head of the bed before walking into the bathroom to get ready for the day.

Mid shampoo, it hits me that we made it through the entire night, and well into the morning without any issues. Maybe Sam is right. Maybe his beacon is helping disguise Hailey's. The beam of hope has butterflies fluttering in my stomach. Without additional thoughts to effect my mood, I finish showering. After getting dressed and brushing my teeth, I decide to forego applying makeup, knowing the heat of the day will just melt it off. Instead, I spend some time scrunching my hair with the towel getting the excess water out, and walk back into the main room.

Hailey still has not moved from the position she was in before I took a shower, so I make an executive decision to let her sleep. I leave a note for her letting her know that I will be back soon, and to text or call as soon as she wakes up. I grab my phone, keys, and wallet before leaving to walk downstairs. Halfway down the stairs, I decide to text Sam to see if he is up yet. As my foot hits the tiled floor at the bottom, I hit send and instantly hear the ding of a text message notification. I look up from my phone and find Sam sitting on a bench in the lobby staring intently at his laptop.

"Why so serious?"

Sam doesn't respond, and I find myself getting frustrated with him all over again. How dare he act like he's the one who is mad. He has no right to be, he's the one who insulted me last night, not the other way around. Forgoing any more attempts at a conversation, I let my nose lead me to food. *Il Macchiato* is the only thing open right now, but the aroma coming from the coffee food bar has captured my attention and has my mouth watering with each step I take in its direction. Pulling out a chair and sitting I look over the menu. With limited options, I opt for the ham and cheese croissant, with an iced latte to sip on while I wait. Pulling out my phone, I scroll through social media for a minute before switching to my weather app. I'm concentrating on the time lapse radar and watching a storm build just off the coast that looks like it will make landfall around three when I feel a familiar presence pull out the chair to my left and sit down. Without looking up from my phone, I know it's Sam who has sat down next to me. After the way the conversation ended last night and how he ignored me this morning, I refuse to be the first to speak. If he wants to talk, he will have to find a way to delicately break the ice.

"Are you going to just sit here and ignore me? Or are you going to get out of your mood from last night?"

"Me get out of my mood?! You are the one who didn't talk to me when I walked up to you earlier, Sam!"

"What are you talking about?"

The waiter sits my food in front of me, with a reminder that it is hot and quickly walks away, clearly not wanting to get in the middle of what has rapidly become a heated conversation.

"When I came downstairs I texted you to see if you were awake and the notification from your phone is what caught my attention. You were in the lobby looking at something on your laptop. I asked you why you looked so serious, and you didn't even bother to look up and acknowledge my presence, much less respond to me. So no Sam, I'm not in a mood from last night. I am in a mood because of you today."

"I swear I didn't hear you or see you Kat. I would have said good morning to you and asked if you wanted to come grab some coffee. I was looking over some documents one of our lawyers sent over, and I guess I just zoned everything, and everyone out."

"Oh."

I don't really have much else to say to that without

sounding like a complete bitch, so I just leave it at that and drop the conversation.

"Are you going to order something?"

"No, I already ate. But I will order another cup of coffee. Is Hailey still asleep?"

"She was when I left the room. Poor kid didn't move an inch while I was getting ready, she is out cold. I left a note for her to text or call when she wakes up. I figured I could bring her breakfast in bed, and while she is eating we can figure out our next move."

"That sounds like a good plan. I'm going to get my coffee to go, and head out to the loungers by the pool. I've got some stuff I still need to finish catching up on. If she's still asleep when you finish eating, meet me out there. We can start a game plan, so that when she does wake up, we don't seem completely unorganized."

Finishing my food, I decide to order a second iced latte hoping that the caffeine will kick start by brain to brainstorm ideas on how to get through the next four days. However, I find myself hitting a mental roadblock. Nothing that I can come up with really pans out long term. Giving in to the momentary frustration, I look at my phone to see if Hailey has messaged me before making my way to the pool.

I see Sam's brown hair just above the top of a lounger as I make my way around the side of the pool. Approaching him, I pick a lounger that faces both Sam and the hotel, ensuring I will see Hailey if she walks on to the balcony. I rearrange the lounger from a laying position by grabbing the head section and lifting it three clicks. Once I have it in the right setting, I test its sturdiness before sitting, just to make sure its not going to collapse back down backwards the moment that I sit down and lean back against it. Satisfied that it is not going anywhere, I get comfortable before filling Sam in on everything that I mulled over last night.

"So I was thinking, after you left, and came up with three options. Number one, what about Key west? We can get a head start on them if we drive down there today. It is at least a three hour drive, so we would have a better sense of them heading towards us than trying to keep tabs of four different people that are somewhere in the city."

Sam thinks on it for a bit before responding, and I can tell he is going over all of the possible scenarios. It's not the worst plan, but it definitely has some faults to it.

"I'm not sure I like the idea of being stuck on an island with the only ways to exit are a boat, or a road that we risk having to pass them on. What's the next option?"

"Option two, we drive and see if they follow us. There are two of us, so as long as we stay ahead of them, we can alternate driving while the other sleeps. We can make our rounds through the Southern Coven and if we find ourselves in trouble, pray we are close to someone you trust."

"I like that plan even less than I do option one. Let's take that one off the table, Kat. Give me the third one."

"The third one is my least favorite, so I'm not sure you'll like it much more than the first. We stay here and keep her hidden. Don't let her leave the hotel room, and one of us will stay on watch at all times."

I can tell the moment the idea leaves my lips that I am right, and that he likes this one even less than the second one.

"You're right, I don't like it either. We're leaving a lot at chance, and that leaves us as sitting ducks. What about using your power to move us timelines? Is that a possibility?"

"Don't you think if that was an option I would have done that every year? Or at least last year in New York? The universe is already angry that we are not where we belong. Moving timelines when we are already out of sync with time is a disaster waiting to happen."

I can't blame him for asking. It's a question I have asked myself a million times over throughout the last few years. The truth is, we don't know what would happen. There are no documented instances in which a witch has continually traveled through time, while already out of their born timeline. If it was just me, I would take my chances and risk the unknown. But I can not chance it with Sam and Hailey. I have been at this far too long to mess up now.

We sit here for what feels like forever just staring at each other, as if that will cause a light bulb to go off above one of our heads.

"This would be a lot easier if we could reach out to some other people, Kat. Bounce ideas off of them, or even go ahead and ask for help protecting her. I'd feel better if we had more men down here who knew what was going on."

"You know we can't do that Sam. Not unless we have no other choices available."

He sighs as he runs his hand through his hair, but I can see the resignation in his eyes. He knows that I'm right.

"Tell me about the men. Tell me what they look like and what you know about them. At least if we have an idea of who's after her. We have a better chance at seeing them coming."

Sam's question catches me completely off guard, and I find myself mentally reaching back into the recesses of memories from ten years ago. Aside from the man that I saw in New York last year, I acknowledge that there is a good chance that the men's appearances have changed drastically over the last decade. Beginning with the man we encountered in New York, I meticulously describe each of them, emphasizing the features that are least likely to change with time.

"All four of the men have fair skin and black eyes. I'm not talking about such a dark brown that they look black, but I truly mean the depths of hell black. The man we encountered in New York is the one that I suspect can teleport. There is no other explanation of how he wasn't there one second, and was right on us the next, seeming to materialize out of nowhere. He had a plain appearance, and nothing really stood out about him, other than being short for a guy, maybe five-foot-nine? I honestly didn't get a good look at him because I was trying to get us away, I think he had gray hair."

I stop mid sentence to look up at our room, swearing I saw someone move in there. Checking my phone to see if Hailey texted, I place it back down and continue on after seeing only my lock screen with no notifications.

"The details I can give you on the other three men is a decade old, and I'm not sure how much has changed about them. One of the men had a distinctive tattoo that ran up his neck and onto a bald head. It was thick black markings, almost tribal-like. He might have hair now, or may even be wearing a hat, but the tattoo on his neck would be unmistakably recognizable if we saw it. One of them had an eye patch and a prominent scar that traveled from his hairline on the right side of his forehead, down and under the patch, and continued all the way down to his chin. The last one boasted bright reddish orange hair and a beard to match. I know that people can dye their hair or shave, but if he hasn't, we would see him coming a mile away. His teeth were shaved down into small points, and his nose looked like it had been broken but never reset."

Closing my eyes, I summon mental images of each of the men from that fateful night, striving to provide the most detailed descriptions possible. Satisfied with the recollections, a sudden high-pitched scream tears through the air, prompting my eyes to snap open in the direction of the sound. A blur of something purple catches my attention as it hurtles from my balcony toward the pool. My eyes and brain struggle to synchronize, causing a momentary delay in processing the unfolding scene. But as soon as they decide to work in unison the realization of what is happening hits me at the exact moment Hailey plunges into the water, narrowly missing the waterfall and steps on that side of the pool. My legs propel me forward before my brain fully registers the urgency, and the next thing I know, I am wading up to my chest in the pool. I reach Hailey the moment that she emerges from the water. With a look of shock on her face she starts coughing up the water from her lungs while she tries to catch her breath.

"What the hell were you thinking? You could have hurt yourself! "

None of this makes sense. Why would she jump from the balcony into the pool, and why didn't she text me when she woke up?

"There was a man in my room! I wasn't feeling well when

I woke up this morning, so I decided to stay in bed and wait for you to get back before getting up and out of bed. When I heard the door open and quietly click shut, I assumed it was you trying to make sure not to wake me. But when I rolled over, it wasn't you, there was a man in the room and he was walking towards me. There wasn't anywhere else for me to go, so I jumped out of bed on the opposite side of the man towards the balcony. When he lunged for me I went out of the sliding glass door on to the balcony. I didn't have any other option but to jump and pray I landed in the pool."

Looking around to find Sam and see if he heard what Hailey just revealed, I find that he is no longer in the lounger he had been in. Glancing around the pool I realize he is nowhere in sight. I look up to the balcony to see if there is someone there, but all I can see is the sheer curtain swaying through the open balcony door. Wrapping my arm around Hailey, and leading her out of the pool, we head over to the lounge chairs that Sam and I had just been sitting in. The bartender that was behind the bar getting set up for the day and who witnessed everything is power walking towards us with towels in his hands. With a concerned look on his face, he asks if we needed anything and if he should call security before walking off to grab us some water to drink. Not wanting to leave Hailey to find Sam, I go to grab my phone from my pocket to send him a text, only to bring out a waterlogged and now dead phone. Frustrated, I toss it off to the side, and look around, finding Sam standing on the balcony that Hailey had just jumped from. Raising my arms up in a questionable motion, he just shakes his head no before disappearing back into the room.

"Hailey, who was the man in your room?"

"I, um... I don't... I don't know. I've never seen him before."

"Are you sure it wasn't one of the men after you?"

"I'm positive. I've never seen this man before. I don't remember a lot about those guys, but I do remember that they were all white and fair skinned. This guy had dark skin, and his eyes were glowing, Aunt Kat. I've never seen anyone's eyes glow before, but his looked like they had some type of light charging them from behind. He was really scary."

"Hailey, I need you to think really hard. Did this man say anything to you? Anything at all, even if it seems insignificant or irrelevant."

"No. He didn't say anything. He was in the area between the bathroom and your bed when I rolled over, and he just kept walking towards me. He never said anything though, not when I saw him, not when he lunged for me, or even when I ran out onto the balcony before jumping."

Putting my feelers out, I can sense the men that are after us are in North Miami, and aren't anywhere near the hotel. Even if they were able to teleport small distances at a time, they would not have been able to make up that much distance in the short amount of time that it has been since Hailey jumped off the balcony to now. Adding to the stress, my paranormal senses fail to pick up any other supernatural presence in close proximity. Nothing makes sense. I stand up and start pacing while trying to put my thoughts together and am relieved to see Sam emerge from the bar area. That is until I notice our backpacks gripped tightly in his right hand, swinging with every step he takes in our direction.

"We need to leave. Now."

His voice resonates with firmness, leaving no room for negotiation. I have never seen this side of Sam before, but I can see why many might be intimidated by him. He is beyond pissed off, and the anger tangibly seeps out of his pores. The muscles in his arms are barely contained by their vast size against the tight green v-neck short sleeve shirt he has on. The vein at his temple is visibly pulsing with every beat of his heart. Everything about him screams danger, and if I did not know him so well, I would be terrified. Hailey and I are both soaked to the bone, her purple sleep shirt clinging to her body, and my maxi dress weighed down by the weight of the water it has absorbed. Following him through the bar and towards the lobby to leave the hotel I ask him if we can stop by the bathroom to quickly change. He allows us the opportunity to change with a warning of urgency. I guide Hailey to the closest bathroom grabbing our bags from Sam, and let him know we will meet him at the front desk. Sam has already checked all three of us out of the hotel, and is waiting by the bathroom door when we emerge from changing.

"We can take my car, it's leased under an alias. I don't trust that yours hasn't been tampered with."

The thought isn't one that had crossed my mind. Every year we have either driven ourselves, or rented a car when we got to our destination, and I never once thought I could be putting us at risk by leaving a paper trail. How could I be so stupid? We follow Sam to his black Audi A4 and pile in without a word.

Siri redirects us seven different time as Sam continues to intentionally take wrong turns, but fifteen minutes into the drive he seems satisfied that we're not being followed and loosens up enough that I feel safe to start asking questions.

"Where are we going?"

"The Keys. Now start talking. Who the hell was that?"

His question doesn't catch me off guard. It's an obvious question. Yet the intensity in his tone and the forcefulness of each word momentarily short-circuits my brain, rendering me speechless. Fortunately Hailey is able to fill in the blanks from the back seat and provide Sam with details based off of our conversation earlier. She reassures him know that the man isn't one of the men that have been chasing us for the past decade, and gives him a detailed description of the man that was in her room.

"What do you mean glowing eyes?"

As I relay to him the information Hailey shared with me earlier, I observe his side profile, noting the subtle scrunch of his eyebrows in response to this unexpected revelation. He shakes his head ever so slightly from left to right as if trying to understand the words coming out of her mouth and make them make sense. Running his left hand through his hair, down the back of his head, around his neck, and along to his jawline back towards his mouth, I can tell that he is frustrated. Without casting a glance in my direction he grabs his phone, presses some buttons and a ringing sound echos throughout the car.

"Who are you calling?"

My words have finally found their way back, and unfortunately they have brought their friends dread and anxiety with them. Sam gives me a side eye, as if I should already know the answer to my question, and it hits me. He's calling for backup. Before I can protest, a males voice fills the speakers.

"Whats up, Boss?"

"I need you to do me a favor. I need you to find something out for me. Find out what type of supernatural has glowing eyes."

"Um. What? Come again."

"Someone out there has eyes that seem to glow from the inside out, and I need to know what they are and who they belong to. I shouldn't have to tell you this, but keep the upmost discretion possible. Don't answer questions you don't have to, and don't talk to people who aren't going to help answer the question. I expect a call back at the top of every hour to let me know how your search is progressing."

Without even saying a goodbye, Sam hangs up the phone and stares straight ahead while continuing to drive. Hailey's head pops up from the back in between Sam and I when she turns to Sam and asks who the guy was on the phone.

"My Second in Command. Why?"

"I don't know, his voice sounded familiar, I just can't place it."

She might not be able to place it right now, but I can. And I know if he shows up here, or she figures it out, all of my work will have been for nothing. Shit.

# 10

# Hailey

It's nearly four in the afternoon by the time we make it to the island of Key West. Aunt Kat fell asleep not long after we began driving, and despite Sam's friend calling every hour as promised, we're still in the dark. The last call that Sam received was to report that they were following a lead from the Midwest Coven out of Minnesota. Sam decides to pulls over at a gas station to top off the tank, and I take the opportunity to use the restroom before heading the rest of the way to the hotel. As I'm walking back through the gas station towards the car, a bag of Cool Ranch Doritos catches my eye and I decide that now is a good time to restock our snack inventory. Grabbing each of us a big bag of chips, some beef jerky, drinks and a few other goodies, I check out and head back towards the car, with a triumphant smile on my face knowing I just hit the holy grail of snacks. The sound of our car door closing as I exit the store steals my attention away from my snack driven thoughts, only to find Aunt Kat still half asleep as she walks in my direction. I hold up the snacks letting her know that I have us covered as we bypass on the sidewalk. Giving me a thumbs up, she continues on towards the bathroom and I make my way back to Sam's car where he's finished pumping gas and is on the phone receiving his hourly update.

"Boss, I gotta ask, what have you gotten yourself into?"

"Just tell me what you found out."

I slide into the passenger seat and listen in as the man on the phone tells Sam that the person in my room is something that he calls a tracker. I give Sam a questioning look, holding out my hands in a questioning manner, and in response he holds up a finger, signaling for me to hold on.

"A tracker? I've never heard of that, what kind of magic does he possess and where does he come from?"

Sam not knowing what this man is, worries me more than I care to admit. From what Aunt Kat has told me, Sam is extremely powerful and a leader of some kind. If he doesn't know what a tracker is, how are we supposed to stay away from him, and why does he want me? Sam must feel my apprehension and anxiety building, because he lays his hand on my shoulder and talks in a softer tone. I listen as he and the other man go back and forth in conversation until Sam ends the conversation telling the other man to get as much information as he can and find out why a tracker might be after someone, just as Aunt Kat makes it back to the car and she shoos me to the backseat.

"So apparently the man that was in Hailey's room today is a tracker. From the intel I just received, trackers come straight from the pits of hell and are able to survive on earth because of demon magic. This explains why we didn't sense him coming. They have the nose of a bloodhound, and it is their sole mission to track down their assigned target. Seeing that the tracker is after Hailey, can either of you tell me why that might be?"

Suddenly the car becomes deafening silent with neither Aunt Kat or myself saying a single word. Sam stares at us, silently waiting for one of us to say something, anything. In typical Sam fashion, his patience runs thin and with an exasperated sigh and small shake of his head, he puts the car in drive. Pulling out of the gas station, Sam heads back in the same direction that we came from, eliciting concerned looks from me and my aunt. The silence becomes unbearable as we pass through yet another red light still heading to the north side of the island.

"Where are we going? The hotel is the other way."

The question wasn't uncalled for, but the look that Sam gives my aunt has me sitting further back into my seat and thanking the lucky stars above that she beat me to the punch.

"Well, since neither of you seem to know how or why we've got a mystery Joe on our tail, we're switching to plan Z. With so much unknown about this guy, I don't want to take any chances. Our coven has safe houses scattered throughout our territory. Each location is kept under a safeguard, and in top secret locations only known by the Coven's top leaders. The wards that protect the house should hold any unwanted visitors at bay, but I'm calling in reinforcements. Before either of you say anything, it is nonnegotiable. We don't know what we're up against and we're not taking changes by doing this alone."

"Sam, I can't stop wondering, what if this guy is working with the other four men? Don't you find it odd that they never ventured to South Miami? They stayed in the north, almost like decoys. You have to admit, it is suspicious."

It's Sam's turn to be quiet now. Sitting in the silence of the car, my aunts words echo in my head. I can't believe that this is happening. It was bad enough when I had four men after me, but now I have to worry about someone else. Someone who can apparently fly under the radar of Sam and Aunt Kat. I break open a bag of chocolate covered donuts that I picked up in the gas station and begin to devour them. I'm a snacker when I'm nervous, and today is not the day to start breaking old habits.

Key West is a small island, so it doesn't take us long to make it back to the north side where the safe house is located. The house, with its unassuming white exterior, comes into view, and the small porch, mostly concealed by a sago palm, gives off an air of complete ordinariness.

"This is the safe house? I hate to burst your bubble Sam, but the house looks a little old and run down... I mean even the storm door looks like it's holding on by its last thread. How is this supposed to keep us safe?"

"It's all about appearances Hailey. The less protected it seems, the less likely anyone will think we are in there. The wards that are in placed on the house will help mask our beacons, and I guarantee the only way any paranormal is getting into the house is if they are invited in."

"Do trackers fall into the paranormal category?"

"I wish I had a real answer for you Hailey, but for now, let's hope so."

Sam's inability to provide a straightforward answer leaves unease festering within me, and the chocolate-covered donuts I devoured earlier seem to be doing somersaults in my stomach. I am a little wary as I cautiously try to open the storm door on the front of the house. It opens with east, and I realize that Sam is right and it's a lot sturdier than it looks. Before I can turn the knob to open the door, Sam whistles at me and motions for me to follow them towards the back of the house. Turning the corner towards the south side of the house, I watch as Sam stops abruptly in front of an inconspicuous old stone bird bath just to the left of the path we're walking on. Out of nowhere a whirring sound fills the air. I look from the bird bath, where Sam has stopped, to the light pole in the adjacent corner of the backyard. I follow the pole up, and locate the source of the sound when a small camera turns facing our direction, capturing us within its frame. Seconds tick by and soon the sound of the camera adjusting is followed by a soft click of the back doors bolt unlocking. Still in disbelief of what I just witnessed, I follow Sam and my aunt into the small house. Expecting the house to smell of stale air from not being used, I'm pleasantly surprised as a combination of patchouli and sandalwood overtake my senses.

"Sam, are you like James Bond or something?"

The question is originally meant as a joke, and it does a great job of breaking the tension that has grown in the short distance from the gas station to this house. My aunt covers her mouth in an attempt to hide her laugh, until Sam chuckles so loud that she snort laughs, triggering a chain reaction that has all of us laughing so hard tears stream down our faces. It's the first moment of normalcy that I've felt since I woke up yesterday morning, and I find myself craving its comfort.

The moment is short lived, and soon enough Sam is apologizing for how small the house is. He proceeds to assign rooms, indicating that my room is down the short hall to the left and Aunt Kat's room is to the right. My face must give off a questioning look as I eye the remaining door, wondering if it is a bathroom because Sam continues on to let us know that he will sleep on the couch. I want to argue that it should be the adults that get the rooms, but the small voice inside my head is telling me to be quiet. The more I think about it, the further away I am from the questionable front door the better.

Walking a few steps down the hallway and stop in front of the door Sam identified as my room. I turn the doorknob and open the door to a very small, plain room. I am not sure what I was expecting but the room is far from spectacular yet inviting. Entering the room there is a comforting woodsy smell with a mixture of vanilla. I close my eyes and inhale deeply as it brings a smile to my face reminding me of the park in Houston after it rains. Opening my eyes I look around the room. There is a bed with a blue duvet cover that is located against the wall in the corner opposite the door to the room. A matching bedside table to the left of the bed with a small white lamp. There is one window in the room located on the wall that the right side of the bed is pushed up against. With the blinds closed there is no sunlight entering the room. I walk over to the bedside table and turn on the white lamp before tossing my backpack onto the bed.

Grabbing the small plastic bag from the convenient store

that is holding our wet clothes from earlier, I leave my room in search of a washer and dryer. The house doesn't have a wash room, and I'm about to give up hope when I peek into the garage and strike gold. Standing in front of me are two beautiful ruby red Samsung front loaders, and I've never seen anything more magnificent in my life.

"If anyone has dirty clothes, get them out now!"

Packing in backpacks instead of suit cases means that we are traveling with limited amounts of clothes, and unlike Aunt Kat, I don't prioritize three hundred pairs of underwear over an additional pair of pants. After this trip though, she might be on to something, and I should probably take her lead on that. Throwing our wet clothes into the washer, I go back to my room and grab my dirty clothes before making my rounds to Aunt Kat and Sam to gather what the need washed. We've got just enough to make a medium sized load, and as I walk back into the garage, I see that Sam has backed has car into it. I throw everything I've gathered into the washer, and as I am adding the lavender scented detergent, Sam opens the door from the house and puts his head through to ask if I will grab the snacks from the back seat of his car. I get the laundry started,then grab the bags of goodies from the car and head back inside the house. Passing through the kitchen, I stop just short of the breakfast table where Sam and Aunt Kat are sitting. Dropping the bags on the counter nearest to the table, I listen to their seemingly heated discussion.

"One of my guys from Georgia, David, is going to come down to help keep an eye on us. He's going to keep a low profile while he's here, and won't be in the way. The house is already crammed with the three of us, so he's offered to stay in the shed outside. He is going to bring us some groceries when he comes down and do any outside errands for us so that we don't have to leave. But until he arrives, we're on our own for food."

"Well I guess it's a good thing that I picked up some stuff at the gas station, and that we've got some of the stuff that Aunt Kat picked up when we got to the hotel too."

Dumping everything out of the bags and spreading them out, I tally up what we've got. We have a smorgasbord of goodies in our possession: Oreo Double Stuffed Cookies, Peanut M&M's, Doritos Cool Ranch Chips, LAY'S Sour Cream and Onion Flavored Potato Chips, Pringles BBQ Crisps, teriyaki beef jerky, Brown Sugar Cinnamon frosted Pop-Tarts, chocolate covered donuts, powdered donuts, almonds, and a few other half or mostly eaten snacks. Conceding that this is our dinner, we each grab something from the pile, and I grab a chair to join the conversation that I interrupted.

"Your aunt made a good point earlier, we need to consider the possibility that these men may all be working together. We don't know how they found the tracker, but it makes sense with how close they got last year, that they would rope in additional help this year."

"You mean to tell me that there is another possibility besides those four men hiring help? Why else would a lunatic be after me?"

There's a long stretch of silence as my aunt and Sam look back and forth between each other, before my aunt sighs and begins speaking.

"Well... another possibility is that with how powerful your blast was this time, that others felt it and someone got the idea to track down the source of the power. It's possible that this man has no connection to your past, and instead is from this timeline."

They sit and wait, both staring at me, with blank expressions. My brain is trying to process what she just explained to me and as I begin to connect the dots in my head, the conclusion that I come to can't be right, it just can't.

"But that would mean—"

"That this guy isn't going to go away after your power settles back down."

A chill runs down my spine and spreads throughout my entire body as she speaks into existence the same conclusion that I came to. How am I supposed to handle this? It was bad enough that we had to worry about four guys showing up once a year trying to kill me, but now there's someone else out there that might be trying to find me for who knows what reason? At least I know what to expect from the other four. I can feel my anxiety building, its invisible force invading my body.

"What do you think he wants? Do you think he wants me dead like the other guys?"

This time it's Sam who speaks up. Putting the beef jerky that he had grabbed earlier down, he turns towards me giving me his full attention.

"Honestly, we're not sure Hailey. There is a lot of unknown floating around right now, and I know that must be overwhelming and unsettling for you. So lets go over what we do know. We know there are four men out there that want to harm you. We know that those four men are headed this way, so they are likely following the direction that our powers went when we left Miami. We know that our powers are masked now, so there is no way for them to be able to tell exactly where we went once the trail goes cold. As long as you stay inside this house, you should be safe from them."

His words are spoken in a low and soft tone, helping to ground me to the facts. Repeating the words 'stay inside, you'll be safe' over and over as a mantra in my head, I can feel its calming effects. For now, I choose to focus on that rather than the unknown. Rolling my chips back up, I set them on the table and excuse myself stating that I'm tired. The sun still hasn't fully set, it's still early evening, but I'm mentally and emotionally exhausted. Walking through the living room, down the hall, and into my bedroom, I'm tempted to just flop down in the bed. Instead, I crawl into it, and over to the window directly above the bed to look out of the blinds. The window faces the back yard, and has the most stunning view of the sun setting. Opening the blinds half way, I find myself lost in the enchanting view of its deep reds, rich oranges, and purple halo. The view has me finally understanding why someone would want to stay up for a sunset or sunrise. I watch until the sky is dark and I can see the stars slowly begin to appear and flicker as if they have a beacon of their own, calling out to me. I am captivated for just a few moments longer. Not bothering to change into a sleep shirt, I climb between the sheets in the shirt and leggings I put on at the hotel after my high dive attempt from the balcony. Before I can fully settle, the weight of exhaustion accumulated over the last two days claims me.

# 11

# Hailey

Dreams... or rather nightmares of being hunted, my friends and family dying to try and protect me, haunt me making sleep nonexistent. Tossing and turning, I finally give up any attempt at decent sleep as the suns rays glide across my face. Rolling over to look at my phone, it's just past seven in the morning. I turn to look at the source of the light realizing that I left the blinds open. Sitting up to close them, I catch sight of something stuck to the window. Getting a closer look, I stop short as I see a piece of paper taped to the outside of the window. After realizing the paper was not there by accident, my eyes focus on the actual piece of paper as I notice someone's handwriting in black ink. I move a little closer to be able to read what it says. The six words written on it leave me unable to breathe. The panic attack comes without warning. Somehow my body jumps into action as I run across the hall to the bathroom, barely making it to the toilet in time before expelling all of the chips and donuts that I ate last night.

In between the retches of bile intruding my esophagus and my body's survival instinct to breathe, the words flash through my head as bright as the Las Vegas strip. On the brink of hysterics, I try to focus less on the words and more on what I remember last night. The note was not there last night as I watched the sunset... I'm sure of it. There is only one other explanation, and it terrifies me. Someone was in the backyard in the last few hours. Is this note meant for me? Did they see me last night with the window open? Did they watch me while I was sleeping? After expelling the last of the contents within my stomach, and feeling there is nothing left in reserve that may decide to make an appearance, I decide it is safe enough to leave the bathroom. I walk back to my room on unsteady legs. The moment I enter the room, my vision tunnels and all I can see is the note in the same place on the window. My already unsteady legs begin to shake ferociously, and I hold on to the window seal with one hand for balance. With my right hand shaking uncontrollably I follow each word on the note.

The words haven't changed since I read them the first time, and I reassure myself that I read them correctly. Certain that I'm not hallucinating, with my legs still feeling like Jell-o, I slowly find my way down the hall, occasionally placing my still shaky hand son the wall for balance. I continue through the living room, to where I can hear Sam and Aunt Kat talking at the kitchen table. Sam is telling her that David picked up her car from the hotel, and returned it to the rental facility before coming down here. He just dropped off the groceries for us a few minutes before she woke up. Their conversation is in a natural tone sounding like a normal day to day exchange, knowing there is nothing normal about this situation. It takes a minute before they register my presence.

"Hey Sweet Girl. Are you feeling alright?"

"You don't look so good."

As they both speak at the same time, I find myself looking back and forth between the two of them noticing not what they said, but that they are both wearing a concerned expression that mirrors each other. Sam usually doesn't show emotion, and the concern on his face tells me just how bad I must really look.

"I... I think they found us."

If I didn't have their attention before, I definitely do now. My words have them frozen in place. Their facial expressions morph from a look of concern to one of total shock. Neither of them move or speak, but their quizzical eyes track me as I sway nervously from one foot to the other. Time stands still as I look from Sam to my aunt and back. Their statue stances begin to make me question reality. Do I really have these powers that they claim that I do? Have I somehow accidentally stopped time? I can feel the monster creeping in and am halfway into a panic attack when the sound of Sam's watch ticking grounds me back to reality and he finally breaks from the trance.

"What do you mean? Who found us?"

The worry in his voice is not something that I have ever heard before. Sam is always the level headed one, the calm in the storm, the man of reason. If anyone can make me feel better about something, it's him. Yet something about the way he asks those questions makes me feel like I need to puke again. Taking a deep breath in an attempt to quiet the monster inside my stomach that continues to try and claw its way out, I try to find my words and form coherent thoughts. I start slowly by telling them about the note on my window, opting to skip over my mistake of leaving the my blinds open. Before I can finish, Aunt Kat is rushing towards my bedroom like she is in a 100-meter dash at the Olympics. Sam opts for the back door leading outside and barrels through it like a mom on Black Friday when the door opens to the store with the best deals. Unsure that my legs will make the trek all the way back to my room, I opt to Stay put where I am. I shift my full weight against the cabinet that I find myself leaning on and slide all the way down to sit on the floor. I sit in silence as I wait for them to come back.

Sam is the first one to return, with the note in his right hand, and his phone up to his ear, held in his left hand gripping it so tight I expect it to break under the pressure. He's barking orders at who I can only assume is David, but there is no sound on the other end of the phone to confirm he is even talking to anyone. Aunt Kat comes back in a frenzy, talking animatedly with her hands but I can not understand what she is saying. Something about my window? My brain is spinning round and round with nothing makes sense. Bending my knees up to my chest, I sit my elbows against them. Holding my head in between my hands, in a feeble attempt to get the spinning to stop, I listen to the conversation happening above me. At this point, Sam is off the phone and telling my aunt that David is checking the security cameras, while Aunt Kat sounds like a broken record asking 'what does this mean?' over and over. In between her repetitious panic, there is a tap-tap-thud-thud noise that I can't place. I register the sound as I lift my gaze from the palms of my hands to see Aunt Kat pacing back and forth where the carpet of the living room transitions to the tile of the kitchen. I notice her tell-tale sign of anxiety, as she gathers all of her disheveled hair to one side of her head. Using her left hand I watch as she starts twisting her hair using her index finger. Her finger moves without effort, around and around, until it reaches the end of her hair causing it to fall against her chest. Her right hand comes at the base of her neck and starts the twisting process in the same manner her left hand had previously completed. These movements continue over and over as she paces. Sam is standing inside the kitchen, just inside the back door with one hand on top of his head, and the other on his hip when his phone alerts him to an incoming call.

"Talk."

Sitting all of the way up, I rest my head back against the cabinet. I listen to Sam's one-sided conversation, while watching my aunt continue to pace. I say one-sided conversation is an exaggeration, all Sam is providing me with from his end is a lot of "uh-huh"s and single syllable grunts. Then out of nowhere he slams his fist against the door frame, causing me and Aunt Kat to jump out of our skin, before ending his phone call without saying goodbye and resting his head in the same spot his fist had just landed.

"There's nothing on the cameras. One second the note isn't there, and the next second it is, without a trace of movement on the cameras. We've got nothing."

His words must break through the fog that my aunt is

in, because she finally stops pacing and starts asking the questions that I've had on my mind, but have refused to acknowledge.

"Do you think it's them? They didn't break in, does that mean the wards are working? Do you think they are trying to scare us, by letting us know that they know where we are and that they can get her at any time? Why would leave a note saying that they want to help her? They are the danger! Do you think it's a sick trick to lure her into a sense of security? How did the security system not pick anyone up?"

Her questions come out in a rush, not giving Sam any time to answer in between them. It makes me wonder if mind-reading is a gift Aunt Kat doesn't realize she has. As I concentrate in order to focus on following all the questions she is asking, I realize they are spot on to the ones spinning around inside my head. The feeling of uneasiness builds as it permeates the air around us, so tangible it feels like it has eliminated all oxygen in the room, making it harder and harder to breathe. Neither of us wanting to hear the answers, yet our only lifeline is knowing the truth. Aunt Kat's questions finally come to an end, only to be proceeded with a stretch of silence. It's the calm before the storm. As my thoughts try to grasp on to anything that makes sense, I realize I have been unknowingly holding my breath and counting in my head to gain control of my anxiety. The silence has me wanting to crawl out of my skin. In an attempt to stop the monster that has begun to grow, I listen for the clock and try to slow my heartbeats to match the tick of its second hand. After two long rotations, I have almost successfully shoved the monster back into the pit that it lives when Sam's sigh breaks my trance and dread sweeps back over me.

"I don't know, Kat. I really just don't know. As far as the security system, I can only guess. The camera is motion activated so my best theory is that they were able to use the cover of one of the trees out there that partially block out the window and get in and out undetected. Maybe they teleported to it, I don't know."

"How would they have known to go to that exact spot?"

"You know I don't like to base a conversation off of "what if's" and scenarios... but we really don't have anything else to go on. I think we need to consider the idea that somehow at least one of them knew the safe house was here. There is a possibility they have staked it out at some point in the last decade, just in case we showed up. It's the only thing that makes sense. I just don't know how our location could have been compromised. No one knows the locations of our safe houses other than myself, my Second in Command, and each of the council members that lead our coven."

"But it's possible, right? It's possible that one of those people gave us up. Is there anywhere else we can go that they wouldn't know about?"

"I guess it's possible, Kat. But if that's the case, then no... there is no where we can go where we would be safe. I think we need to sort out a few things privately, and see if that gives us any clarity on our next steps."

Taking my cue to leave, I wiggle my toes to make sure that my legs are going to work with me and not against me. After slowly and successfully standing up, I grab a pack of Pop-Tarts out of the box sitting on the counter, and walk back to my room. If they want to talk without me present, it's fine by me. The unknown of everything is only making me more nervous, and I'd rather wait to hear what's going on, once they have a solid game plan in place. Grabbing the small notebook that I carry in my backpack and my satchel of pens, I sit on the bed and start to journal. Writing down my thoughts is something that I've found helps to calm me down over the years, and I'm hoping that today is no different. As I open the notebook to the first available blank page, I decide I want to start with writing out my concerns. Grabbing the blue glitter pen from the selection of colors, I start listing them out. But rather than finding a soothing pattern and relief in getting the concerns out of my head and onto paper, I find myself answering each concern with more lingering questions. Flipping the page over, and exchanging the blue glitter pen for a deep red pen, I change my approach and start writing down the unanswered questions that plague my mind. Finding a groove, I fall into a hypnotizing pattern where each question begs to ask another, and when I finally review my work, I realize that I have three pages worth of questions along with a knot in the pit of my stomach. Something doesn't feel right, yet I can't quite put my finger on what it is. Reading each question over and over, line by line, I decide to make the ones that disturb me the most with a star in the left margin next to the question. Once completed, I now have a list of five starred items. Knowing the areas that bring me the most concern and unease, I put my pen and paper down. Closing my eyes, I start from the beginning, trying to recall every detail that I can from the night they broke in. The nightmare that has repeatedly haunted me for the past decade comes to my imagination with ease. Playing it over in slow motion, I study the details and pick it apart scene by scene, second by second. I've never given it so much focus. Normally I'm trying to claw my way out of it, and it leaves me shaken. Replaying it over in my mind, I watch as the door is kicked in, and I'm thrown backwards into the table. I watch as the men enter the house in orderly fashion, guns aiming forward and moving side to side searching for their target, before two men take aim towards the kitchen where my mom is, and another towards Aunt Kat. I watch intently as the fourth man turns towards me, dropping his gun to his side before rushing in my direction. Rewinding the scene again, I play it even slower, making sure my mind isn't playing tricks on me. Shots are fired towards the kitchen, another shot is fired in the direction of my aunt, but she's on the move racing in slow motion towards me. The man with the tattooed head and neck turns his body in the direction of where I land, his eyes tracking the movement of my aunt before turning and making eye contact with me. I watch as he takes long strides in my direction, trying to get to me before my aunt does. He lowers the gun inch by inch with each microsecond that passes, raising his unarmed hand towards me. Aunt Kat's hand grabs my wrist just before he reaches me and the scene goes black. I assumed that I had passed out at this point and that's why everything my nightmare always goes black here, but now I question if this is the moment we left that timeline. Opening my eyes, and looking back down at my paper, I underline the two questions that disturb me the most, and add two new ones.

★ *The men have guns. If they wanted me dead, couldn't they have just shot me through the window last night?*

★ *Why didn't they kill me when they broke into our house? They clearly had training with guns and had every opportunity to.*

*—Is the note true? Are they trying to help me? From who, the unknown man? Or is that man working with others to save me from the four men that broke in that night?*

*—What if my whole life is a lie?*

I've never questioned anything as much as I am right now. I know that my aunt tends to lean towards a 'need to know basis' when it comes to our history and past events, but she wouldn't lie to me... would she? Every question I ask myself, only raises more questions in return, and I find myself going down a never ending rabbit hole, unable to pull myself from its out-of-control spiral.

# 12

# Sam

Kat and I have been staring at each other for almost thirty minutes, getting no where in our discussion. Tired of the push back, I decide it's time to be blunt.

"Kat, I'm going to be real honest with you right now, and I need you to be honest with me. I know that there is information that you're still hiding, and you've been hiding since day one. Normally, I don't say anything to you about it and I let it slide. I know you have your reasons, and I understand that you are only trying to protect yourself and Hailey, but I think, at this point, we are past your gate keeping of information. As leader, I am responsible for the safety of my coven, which includes you and Hailey. If I'm going to be successful, then I need to be let in on everything."

Nothing that I've said, up until this point, has gotten through to her, but I can tell something just did. I watch as her jaw clinches and her lips tighten into thin lines in the 'I'm not giving you an inch' facade that I know so well. Watching her closely, her next move will indicate if I have made any positive progress. Seconds tick by when I notice the small twitch in her right cheek, she closes her eyes together longer than normal and when she opens them to take a deep breath, I see the sign I am looking for. Simultaneously, her mouth goes slack and she hunches into herself every so slightly. If I was not looking for it, I would have missed it, because in one more breath she straights her spine, puts on her game face and looks me directly in the eye waiting for me next strategic move. Kat isn't one to go down without a fight, so any give that I can get, I'll mark as a win in my favor. Taking this as my que, and not waiting a second more in fear she'll close back up, I start with a single question, knowing that she's a ticking time bomb and needs to be handled with care.

"I think the best question to be answered right now is, what year are y'all from?"

"I do not see how knowing that is going to help."

"It will give us an idea of what, and possibly who, we're up against, Kat. Are y'all from the past, where it's possible someone knew of y'all then, and has just been waiting around for y'all to show back up? Are y'all from the future, where no one here would know y'all, and this random Joe is either a coincidence or possibly connected to the original four? You've got to give me something to work with here."

"Fine, Same, we are from the future."

It takes me a moment to process what she as finally revealed. I don't know why her words surprise me. Maybe deep down I just assumed they were from the past, after all traveling, back in time carries higher risks. Or maybe I never thought I would get the answer to the question I've been asking for the last seven years. A thought occurs to me, giving me a glimmer of hope.

"Okay. Then, I guess my next sensible question would be, how far in the future are we talking? Is there a possibility of us running into the you or Hailey of... umm... 'this time'?"

"Sam, do you understand how dangerous that would be? She can not be in the same time and space as another version of herself. So no, you won't run into a little Hailey skipping down the sidewalk of Canal Street if you decide to go and grab some ice cream on a random Tuesday."

Her unwillingness to share exact details doesn't go unnoticed, and neither does her mention of Hailey's inability to be in the same time span, but no mention about herself.

"Alright, Hailey can't, but what about you?"

I can hear the the sound of my watch ticking with each passing of the second hand. Kat's silence is all the answer that I need, yet I find myself wanting... needing to hear her say it. She's not one to trip up on her words, or let you know more than she intends, but by the look on her face, I can tell she knows she screwed up. Growing frustrated as I attempt to wait her out, with light bulbs steadily going off in my head left and right, I throw in the towel along with my patience.

"You're telling me that Hailey doesn't exist here, but you do? Because that's what I'm gathering from your silence. Kat, the silence that you love so much isn't protecting y'all anymore, and I'm beginning to think of it as an admission of guilt."

"Sam, you don't understand—"

"No, you're right. I don't understand, Katherine. You are

the reason I don't understand. I am here to help, and open to anything you tell me, yet you are still being guarded. Let me see how well I understand your silence... you're telling me that Hailey's parents are out here somewhere? Possibly the key to everything about her, and you're just choosing to keep that little nugget to yourself? What exactly do you plan on doing when Hailey is born in this timeline and then there are two of them? Do you have a plan for that? I'm not playing these games anymore Kat, you need to start talking, and now."

"I don't know Sam, I don't have any set plans. I went backwards in time because I thought that if I had a do over, I could save us all. I did not mean to go a full ten years back, but I guess in the rush of everything, when I teleported us, the memory I latched onto was from 2006. Hailey does not possess the ability to manipulate time, so she is stuck here until time catches up to itself. I couldn't change out timeline again even if I wanted to. There's a reason that messing with time is so dangerous. Because we moved backwards, if she runs into herself, her entire timeline would collapse, and she would cease to exist. I know where I was during this time, so I can avoid myself and I can help her avoid herself too, once she is born. But Sam, we can not tell her any of this. If she knows that her mom and her dad are out there somewhere, she is going to go in search of them. We can not risk her changing the course of things before it's time. She will put us all at risk."

Her words strike me as genuine, she was trying to save her best friend, and my heart hurts for her. Time traveling is not something I have the ability to do, so I don't have a lot of knowledge on it. From the little studying that I've done on it though, her words ring true. I've read things and heard stories about people who get stuck in time, or who die while attempting to manipulate time. Usually it's people who are attempting a skill they don't possess, with the help of some dark magic, but I can see the parallels to Hailey. She doesn't possess any abilities at the moment, so it would make sense that she would be bound by the same rules of those tinkering with magic that doesn't belong the them. I know Kat is right as well, and that we can't tell Hailey any of this. Scrubbing my face with my hands partially out of frustration, and partially in a acknowledgment, I let her know that I agree, Hailey can not know.

"We need a game plan Kat, and that includes me knowing everything. Start from the beginning, and leave no stone un-turned."

I sit quietly and listen as Kat finally opens up. As she is talking, I begin making mental notes and creating an internal check list of things that I need to follow up on. I listen as she tells me that Hailey was born in April of 2017 in Louisiana. Mentally I note that I have one year to find her parents before remembering a vital piece of information that she has openly shared since I met them. Hailey's dad died before she was born.

"I hate to interrupt, but I remember you saying that Hailey's dad died before she was born. Do you know exactly when he died?"

"Oh. Um, no. Her mom told me that he passed before she was ever able to tell him that she was pregnant. He never even knew that Hailey existed. Look, I know where you are going with this. You want to track her parents down, find out more about Hailey and all of that. But I am telling you Sam, I have spent the last ten years looking for her mom and haven't had any luck. I have poured countless hours scouring social media. I have gone down a rabbit hole of public records from births in multiple states and counties looking for a bread crumb. I have even hired a private detective at one point. It is to the point that I have questioned if her identity was even real, because I'm telling you Sam, she's a ghost. Do you know how hard it is to track down someone you know nothing about until a future date? I finally gave up and just plan to bide my time until the first time that I met her, when I know exactly where she will be, and I can track her from there."

She's right, again. Tracking down someone we know little to nothing about isn't going to be an easy feat. However, Hailey's dad would have had to have been pretty powerful to create an offspring as powerful as she is. Every coven keeps a list with each of its members and any special powers they possess. Assuming that her dad was born into and baptized by a coven, there will be a record of him somewhere. I make another mental note to check our census records and birth records, and cross reference them with any males that are on the known list to possess additional powers.

"How old was Hailey's mom?"

"She was twenty-five when she had Hailey, why?"

Ignoring her question, I add an age range between twenty to forty for Hailey's dad's description. We may not know who he is yet, but we now have more to work with than we do for Hailey's mom. If Hailey was born in Louisiana, there's a good chance that's where her dad was from. If not there, then at least the Southern Coven, which means we may not have to involve anyone else. The less people who know that we're looking for someone, the better.

"I'm sorry, I didn't mean to interrupt, keep going."

Giving her head a little shake from left to right, she starts back where she left off. I continue to listen without interrupting her again, making small notes to myself as she goes on. I can feel her exhaustion by the end of her story, as well as a deep sense of regret. Without her having to say or admit it, I can tell she blames herself for everything that happened that night. Her regret is palpable through every detail she has lived and relived the last ten years. From not recognizing the implications of Hailey's powers, along with not sensing the men approaching sooner, and ultimately the death of her best friend.

The sound of the washing machine finishing the load that I rewashed this morning is barely notable as it dings. Needing a moment to think everything over that I just learned, I excuse myself to go swap over the clothes from the washer to the dryer, leaving Kat at the table alone. It doesn't take long to switch the load over to the dryer, but instead of going back inside immediately after, I walk over to the car, quietly opening the door, before sitting down in the passenger seat. Closing the door with extra caution to make sure that I can't be heard, I grab my phone, pull up J's number and without hesitation hit send. The phone doesn't complete a full ring before I hear his familiar voice on the other end.

"Hey Boss, what's up?"

"Hey, do me a favor. Can you go through our census and birth records for the last twenty to forty years? Narrow it down to all male births, who at the time of maturity exhibited additional powers. Start in Louisiana, and if you strike out there, look at the other states in our coven."

The sound that comes through the other end of the earpiece has me pulling my phone away from my ear , until the high pitched whistling is finished, before placing it back.

"That's a big favor Boss. Any way that we can narrow it down some more?"

"I know it is. You can probably narrow it down to men who are currently single. I don't think the guy we're looking for is married, but you never know. Actually, go ahead and still pull them, but put married males on a separate list. If we strike out with single guys, then we'll move to that list. Prioritize them by how much power they possess. I don't think we're looking for a person who's bound to using spells out of a book. We're looking for someone who has powers strong enough to exhibit something big like telekinesis or astral projection."

"Alright, got it. I gotta ask though, first you tell me to have a bag packed and ready to go in case you need me in Florida, then you need me to find out information on a tracker. Now you need me to find information on an unknown guy who may or may not be part of our coven. Is this about that energy surge that we all felt a few days ago?"

"Umm... yeah, it kind of is. It is of utmost importance that you do not say a word to anyone. Keep this on the down low. I don't wait to raise any flags for anyone else unless we need to. David is down here with us, and is good to stay and help keep an eye on things until we can come back. I'm thinking that we'll be able to start driving back Monday evening, stop mid way to make sure that we aren't being followed, and head the rest of the way Tuesday. I'm going to get them settled back in Houston, and then I'll meet you in New Orleans and help with the search."

"You ever going to let me meet them? You've kept them hidden from the rest of the coven like your dirty little secret, but you talk about them all the time. Shouldn't I at least get to meet the people that are causing me so much work?"

I know that he's joking, but it rubs a raw spot in my chest. I've been so protective over Kat, and especially Hailey, that I've never once considered allowing any of my junior officers to get anywhere close to them, until now. Even with David here, he's under strict protocol to stay out of the house, and out of sight. Maybe once things settle back down, I'll introduce the three of them, but for now I need to focus on keeping Hailey and Kat safe.

# 13

# Hailey

It's funny how quiet a day can be when you sit in your room stewing all day. My mind finding itself in a battleground of decisions and revelations while the world outside seems to hush, almost as if it senses the gravity of the thoughts consuming me. I feel caught in a web spun from secrets as my mind does a delicate dance of what to do with this newfound knowledge, the words etching themselves into the recesses of my brain. I didn't stay to hear the whole conversation, in fear of being caught eavesdropping, but I heard enough. Trips to the bathroom and kitchen have become strategic maneuvers, timed to perfection to avoid any confrontations. My aunt is correct on one thing, now that I know my mom and dad are alive in this time period, I want nothing more than to find them. I've spent the entire day stuck in a cycle between pacing around my room, and scribbling in my notebook, the ideas flowing like a river of ink onto the pages. The pages themselves having morphed into a canvas for my hopes and uncertainties, a testament to the chaos that courses through my veins.

No matter which cycle I am stuck in, one undeniable truth remains. My mom and dad are still alive right now. The notion of this wraps around me like a lifeline, a fragile connection that I am determined to seize and a maddening debate rages within me on my best option to find them. I could make a run for it now, but considering someone is after us and they know where we are right now, I'm not sure that's the best idea. I could wait until after we get back to Houston, and then leave to search for them. The questions isn't weather I will do it, but how. Both of those ideas are problematic and have their risks, but now I also have to take into account that I have powers that can be tracked by Sam, Aunt Kat, and whoever else. Sneaking away won't be a walk in the park.

Knowing I have yet to come up with a logical plan, I throw myself onto my bed, its familiar embrace a refuge from the storm within me. Shoving my face into my pillow I yell as loud as I possibly can. The scream releases me of my pent up anxiety, leaving me breathless and strangely empowered. Turning over onto my back, I gaze up to the ceiling and like a beacon cutting through fog an idea hits me. We were from Louisiana prior to us traveling to this time. Threads of my past intertwine with Sam's, his roots stretching back to the same area that my journey began. Would it be possible for us to move back? I find myself playing out all of the scenarios that my mind can conjure while my fingers mindlessly dance over the sheets as if mapping out the path. Could I convince them though? The question hovers over me like a fragile bubble ready to pop at the slightest inconvenience. Maybe, just maybe, if I can come up with the right narrative. I could play it off as wanting to be closer to more people in the coven, to learn from those who share our powers as I wait on my own to take effect. If I can get them to agree, then I can start looking for my parents. My heart flutters at the possibility that I could be retracing my parents footsteps, walking the same streets they walk, breathing the same air. Doing the math, I should be conceived around July or August. I'm pretty sure that my mom was already living in New Orleans at the time that she got pregnant, so that gives me three months to find them. As I continue to go over the scenarios in my mind, the room around me transforms from a prison of indecision to an open space of possibilities. The world outside remains a mystery, but in this moment I have a tangible plan and I feel like I can finally breathe.

A familiar scent begins to permeate the room, one that tugs at my senses like an old friend, and it only takes me a second before I can place it. Aunt Kat is cooking, and from the smell of things is burning something yet again. Eating dinner with them would mean having to navigate a maze of conversations, and I'm in no mood to talk to either of them. So instead of leaving my room and heading towards the kitchen to ask if they need help, I put my headphones on and lose myself in the music I've downloaded on my phone. I'm four songs in, the music having become a distant echo that tugs at the edges of my conscience, when a new sensations seeps in. The smell of smoke coming from down the hall appears to be getting worse instead of better. The smell is so strong it is going to take more than Aunt Kat waving a dishtowel to get the smoke out, and a pang of concern nudges me. Wondering what exactly Aunt Kat could have burned this time I decide it is time to get out of bed and go help them air out the house.

Sitting up on the edge of the bed I slide my feet into my shoes as movement at my door catches my attention. Not sure that I'm seeing things correctly, I do a double take and see that smoke is starting to seep into my room from the open space between the bottom of the door and the floor, like fog in a scary movie. Prying off my headphones, their departure gives way to a subtle crackling sound. Not loud enough to discern what's making it, but enough to peak my curiosity as to what it is and instinct propels me to my feet to go see what Aunt Kat has gotten herself into. I'm three steps away from my closed door when the heat radiating from the other side has me stopping in my tracks. The aroma of burning continues to grow and the all too familiar Monster begins to take hold in my stomach. This isn't just another burnt casserole. The weight of reality sinks in as I take in my surroundings, the atmosphere itself turning sinister. Frozen like a statue in my own skin, the ability to inhale and exhale begins to slowly fade, depriving me of any oxygen left in the room. Paralyzed in my own fear and my feet cementing me to the ground, I can't formulate an escape plan. Just as the words '*this is it*' play on repeat in my head, a loud sound has the Monster momentarily retreating back into itself. Struggling to pull myself from the trance, another bang comes from behind me and has me dropping to the floor and a scream threatening to escape my lips.

The smoke is turning into an impermeable haze impeding

my ability to see across the room, but Sam's voice pierces through the veil as he yells from outside the house. Intermittent thunderous crashes interject themselves between Sam's words and I imagine he is outside throwing something heavy against the window trying to break it so he can get me out. Recalling the fire drills that we did in elementary school, I follow instinct and stay on my knees. With a quick and desperate motion, I pull my shirt over my nose creating a feeble filter against the putrid smell of smoke, and begin to feel the floor with my hands as I crawl towards the far wall the window is on. Making sure to keep myself out of the possible trajectory of glass when the window looses its war against Sam's strength and whatever he is beating it with, I stay to the lower left side of the wall and curl my body into itself. The glass above me shatters and I can see the smoke start to billow out of the now open window, a symbol of salvation weaving a dance of destruction as it seeks the same escape as me. Sam yells for me to continue to stay out of the way as something resembling a stick comes through the window. As he works to clear the remaining glass from the edges of the window, I stay safety tucked in the corner of the room.

"Hailey, come on!"

With trembling limbs, I rise from my sheltered corner and move to the window. As I get closer I see Sam hand a rake over to my aunt, and my pulse quickens as he retraces his steps towards me, his face a mask of determination. Using the bed for leverage, I lean over towards the window and wait for Sam to grab my hands to help me through. Just before he reaches me, a shiver ripples down my spine. Something in Sam's eyes shifts, and his face contorts, alarm etching itself into its features. In a fraction of a second a pair of arms materialize out of the corner of my eye, and I'm trapped in their unyielding embrace from behind. In a desperate attempt to flee, I pivot towards Sam. My foot slips off of the edge of the bed causing me to lose all leverage and the arms hoist me into the air. Panic surges in my chest as my feet dangle in the air, searching for the floor, bed, or anything that will give me the upper hand on my assailant. The vise-like grip around my waist tightens and I can hear Sam and my aunt yelling in alarm as everything around me becomes fuzzy. I can feel my body being pulled backwards, before turning and moving forward. My senses blur as reality warps around me. Everything around me streaks by in a frenzied dance of lights and shadows, suspending me in an alternate realm where time stands still as the world around me moves.

Abruptly everything stops and I'm standing in the middle of the street watching the house I was just in go up in flames. As I try to focus on the house, vertigo grips me and my surroundings spiral again before stopping and dumping me out at the end of the street. The realization hits me like a lightning bolt. I am the one in motion. Battling a surge of nausea and dizziness, I begin to struggle against the man who has me trapped in his arms. Catching him off guard before he can move us again, his grip loosens and my feet hit the ground. Adrenaline courses through my veins knowing that I don't have a second to spare. With urgency fueling me, I pull my elbow back as hard as I can, hitting him in the stomach. Hearing him grunt, I don't waste another second and take off running as fast as my legs can carry me, pounding the pavement in a staccato rhythm.

My flight is cut short, not making it a full house down the road when he materializes in front of me, an obstruction that I can't sidestep in time. With momentum on my side, I'm propelled directly into his unyielding chest, the collision robbing me of breath and control. Before I can turn around, he grips me around my waist and throws me over his shoulder like a sack of flour. I begin kicking and twisting in an attempt to loosen his hold, but the force of moving again freezes all of the muscles in my body. I'm thrust through the night, each jarring transition magnifying the rolling tempest within my stomach. We move three more times, each time increasingly making me nauseous. Resolve washes over me as I push down any bile that attempts to rise and I study my captors movements with a new found focus. Time becomes both my ally and my enemy as I begin to get a feel for the timing of his movements and mentally etch notes into my memory each time the world halts and resumes with a jagged jolt.

Five is my answer. I have five seconds of perpetual movement in which I'm frozen, before I have a breath of a second to move. I take time to notate that he has my legs held down with one hand, and his other hand is anchored securely around my waist keeping me both in place and unable to kick him. However, my upper body remains tantalizingly free. I wait one more time, and count the five seconds, a rhythm I've measured in heartbeats. One. Two. Three. Four. Five. The world stops streaming by, and before he can move again, I twist my upper body to the left, throwing myself off balance, and off of his shoulder. I'm not sure how I thought this was going to play out. Maybe that I could spin myself off of him, onto the ground and take off again? That would have been best case scenario. Unfortunately I underestimated the grip that he has on my lower half and the ground rushes towards my face, inevitably colliding with helplessness. My arms are too slow to come out from the space between me and my captor. I have no time to brace and split second decision sends my head veering sideways in an attempt to save my face from the brunt of the attack. The side of my head hits the ground, and a searing pain dances behind my eyes, a symphony of light and darkness, before my vision goes completely black.

# 14

# Hailey

"If she gets out of here, she's going to die."

The words register from a distance, each syllable a drumbeat hammering against my throbbing head. I want to move, to curl into myself and nurse the pounding ache, but I don't want to give away that I'm awake. Straining to keep my body motionless and my breathing measured, I try to get a sense of my surroundings. The air around me isn't stale but it doesn't smell like outside either, and I'm laying on either carpet or a rug, definitely inside. I can feel that my ankles and thighs are firmly bound together, and my arms are immobilized, drawn tightly behind me. While I can't move to check, I'm pretty sure they have me in a hogtie position. Muffled voiced fill the air and I strain to count the voices. Three maybe? No make that four. Four people are talking, which tells me that the men who have been stalking me for the past decade are likely the ones who have me. I try to remember any details from the man who grabbed me, but his face was draped in a black ski mask, which when I think about it is odd. Why would someone who I've seen previously try to hide their identity now? Getting out of my head and trying to listen to what they are saying, I hone my hearing into the conversation.

"Did you have to burn the house down?"

"It was the only way to get to her. They had so many wards on the house, that the only way in was if something was opened. He did the job when he busted the window to help her out, and I was able to teleport in."

The verbal exchange goes back and forth like a tense duet, the two men's voices recounting the events that led up to my capture. With caution on the forefront of my mind, I open my eyes just a sliver and try to get a good look at them. All four men are sitting at a dining room table across the room, with animated hands that are flailing around as they speak. Two of them have their back to me, and the others are directly in front of them. By the way that the black masks are scrunched up at the top of the two men who face away from me, I can tell that they've got their masks lifted off of their face. Unable to see enough to identify any of them, I close my eyes again before I get caught, and continue to listen.

"He's going to kill us, you guys do realize that right? He is going to absolutely murder us."

"I know. We need to wake her up. Maybe if we explain things to her she'll listen, and stop trying to run away. She needs to know who she is and why she's in danger. We don't have long before they find her here, and we can't be here when they do."

"Yea, well if you wouldn't have lost her in New York, we

wouldn't be in this predicament would we? We could have dealt with her then, and wouldn't be running the risk of him finding us now. But no, someone let them get on a damn subway train, and now he's traveling with her. I can't believe that you got in and out without him recognizing you."

"You're right, but it was a risk we had to take. Look, I'd love to stay, but now that I got her here, I think that y'all can handle the rest. I need to go before questions start being asked."

The four men go back and forth making it hard to differentiate which voice belongs to who, when ultimately the man I've deemed as "number one" gets up to leave. Slightly opening my eyes again, through the shadow of my eyelashes I steal a glimpse of his departing features. He's short in height, maybe five foot eight or nine, and has a stocky build. I can't see his hair due the mask sitting on top of his head, but has he turns I can see a back beard jet out from his chin. Comparing him to the men who continue to sit at the table, I am confident that this is the man who took me. Closing my eyes again, I hear a door open, and the definitive click of it closing and the deadbolt turning in place. The rubbing of chairs moving against carpet has me on high alert and I can sense the men moving closer to me. Feeling their presence, a chilling realization settles over me as a knee pops audibly in front of me. My eyes widen with a surge of urgency, my mouth preparing to unleash a scream that claws at my throat. Before a sound can escape, a hand clamps firmly over my mouth

"Shh. Don't yell, we aren't going to hurt you. We just need to talk to you, do you understand?"

Fear clutches me in a vice-like grip, rendering my body

immobile, every fiber trembling as if held captive by invisible chains. Even though they have their masks back on, I am certain that these men are the ones who have been hunting me for the past decade. My mind swirls with disbelief. How do they expect me to believe that they wont hurt me? The note left on my window flashes across as a memory, and I start to connect it with the memories of that first night and them lowering their weapons before coming towards me, and again tonight, no weapons around. Who ever left the note on my window had clear sight of me that night and was capable of ending my life right then and there. The guy who took me tonight, could have killed Sam and my aunt and let me burn in the house, or killed me while I was knocked out cold. Is it possible that they don't want to hurt me? My gut is saying that they don't, but everything that my aunt has told me over the past ten years tells me that they do. Against all reason, I choose to follow my gut. A minuscule nod, imperceptible yet profound, manifests as a fragile offering, a concession to the possibility that they may not be the relentless predators I've long perceived.

"Okay, I'm going to remove my hand from your mouth, but you can't scream. Deal?"

Nodding my head again, he slowly removes his hand as if he anticipates that I'm going to scream that he'll need to be close by to cover my mouth again. Relief floods his face when he decides that I won't scream, and he rolls backwards on his heels to sit on the floor in front of me. In an attempt to sit up myself, I confirm what I had already suspected, and that my arms and legs are hogtied together.

"Can you cut that back rope?"

Guy three, his stature commanding a presence despite his shorter frame, emerges from behind guy two, the one now sitting in front of me. His eyes, cloaked in the same obscurity of the masks they all wear, fixate on guy two for a few seconds before shrugging his shoulders and walking my way with a knife that he's pulled out of his back pocket. The blade gleams dully in the ambient light and each step he takes is measured, a calculated progression toward me, marked by the rustle of fabric and the faint creaking of the floor beneath his weight.

"If you say so."

The moment the rope that once bound my hands to my ankles is relinquished, a wave of relief sweeps over me. Sitting up, I and scoot myself back against the wall behind me. The silence is palpable as I work up the courage to speak. I sit there for a moment, my gaze traveling from one man to the next, as I get a good look at the three men in front of me, etching their details into my memory. First, I fix my attention on the man I've designated as number two, seated in front of me. His features, partially concealed by the mask, are a patchwork of obscurity and glimpses. My gaze then shifts to number three, a figure positioned slightly to my right, his body a mixture of height and power contained within a more compact frame. Finally, my eyes alight on number four, still seated at the table, his chair pivoted to give him an unobstructed view of me. Their eyes, pools of unrelenting darkness, are a common thread that bind them. Upon a closer examination of number two I realize that they are contacts. Why are they going to such great lengths to hide their identity now?

"What's with the masks? I've seen your faces before, why hide them now?"

"We can't risk you knowing what we look like now. Things have changed, and we can't take a chance that you or anyone else figures out who we are. Hailey, you're life is in danger. We need to keep you safe."

"What do you mean my life is in danger? I've been running from y'all! You guys were the threat to my life. If it's not you, then who is it?"

Guy one looks over to number two and nods his head as if giving him the signal to take over.

"We don't know. It's always different. We just know that if you don't keep yourself safe, you're going to die. Hailey, do you know what you are?"

"What do you mean it's always different? Can you see in the future or something? And I don't know, I guess I'm a witch or something. I mean, my aunt and Sam can feel my power, and that's how it works right? You can only feel the powers of someone who shares the same type of magic as you?"

"Hailey, when your dad dies, all hell breaks loose, but you have enough power to take over everything. I don't mean lead a coven or a small faction. I mean you have the power to merge all the covens under one leader. Some people saw that as a threat and planned to kill you that night. That's why we came, you weren't safe in that house. Then that lady took you into another time, and we've made it our mission to find you ever since. Last year when we almost caught up to you in New York we knew that we would need to change the way we've been going about this. So we left detailed messages for our future selves to find. Instead of waiting for the barrier to open, we've been trying to track you for the past few months in this time. We started in New York and went to all of the other states that we knew you had been in. We were at the boarder of Georgia and Florida when your power surge swept through and were able to follow its path. "

"Okay, if you're here to supposedly save me, then why hide your face? Why not just talk to my aunt or Sam and tell them that you're on our side? None of this makes sense."

"We don't know who we can trust. Hailey, your dad put us in charge of your safety before he died, but someone betrayed us and we don't know who."

"What do you mean he put you in charge of my safety? My mom never got a chance to tell my dad that she was pregnant, he never knew I existed!"

Before the man has a chance to say anything else, the front door is thrown open, and standing inside the frame is Sam. Number four, who hasn't moved from his chair up until this point, and who is closest to the door, stands up and runs straight for him.

"SAM!"

My voice erupts without warning, a primal instinct to protect Sam from the danger that unfolds before my eyes. My words fall silent as I watch Sam rear back with a swift, and ferocious punch that finds its mark on the man's nose. I can hear the bone chilling crunch of it breaking and watch as he falls to the ground. The one I've labeled as number three, standing to the right, seizes the opportunity and takes off towards the back door as the one sitting in front of me stands to do the same. Number three makes it to the door, pulling it open and darting outside with number two right on his tail. Sam fingers fasten around number two's arm, and with a knife in his right hand, Sam swirls the guy around bringing the blade down, leaving a jagged mark across the mans face. The man wrenches himself free of Sam's grasp with a frantic yelp as he grabs the right side of his face and bolts out of the open door. Turning to where he left the first man in a heap on the floor, Sam sees that at some point number four made an escape and is no longer there. Breathing in deep ragged breaths, and the veins in his neck distended, Sam turns and gets his first good look at me.

"Where's the other one?"

"He left, before you got here."

His shoulders give some slack, and he walks over to me, motioning for me to turn around so that he can untie my arms. Once my arms are free, I'm able to help him untie my thighs and ankles.

"Are you okay? Did they hurt you? What happened to your head?"

"No they didn't, I'm okay, I tried to get away when one of them was carrying me and fell head first on to the ground. What happened?"

"Come on, lets get out of here in case they come back. We'll talk more in the car."

Standing up, the pounding of my head protests, but I push through and follow Sam out of the now nonexistent door and towards a silver car in front of the house. The headlights beam a cascade of light in front of the car, and I expect to see someone waiting in it, but it's empty.

"It's Davids. He took off trying to follow the man who grabbed you, but when he lost the trail, he called and told me where his keys were. Luckily the shed was far enough behind the house that it wasn't touched by the fire. Your aunt stayed behind to talk to the fire marshal and the cops. I came for you."

As if sensing the questions that were on my mind, he's answered them all in the steps between the house and the car. Sliding into the passenger seat, the car is still on as if Sam threw it in park and ran straight to the house. The cool air blowing from the vents is a nice change from the hot humidity of the air outside. After closing my door for me and making sure that I am secure, Sam walks around the car and slides into the drivers side. The car is a standard, and I watch as Sam does the whole shift, clutch, gas thing and gets us moving forward.

"They didn't hurt you?"

"No."

"I don't understand. These guys want you dead, and they had every opportunity to do so tonight. No offense, but why didn't they?"

"They said they were trying to protect me."

Sam's face scrunches into a quizzical state, as if he's questioning everything that he knows and has been told.

# 15

## Sam

It's been just over three months since we were in Florida, and I'm no closer to finding Hailey's mom or dad than I was when we were there. Despite J's diligent efforts to compile a list of potential candidates for her father, no one matches up. The list has become a maze of contradictions and dead ends. We've pored over it exhaustively, accounting for every possible scenario, even those involving married men, yet we remain without leads. The urgency has intensified with the knowledge that Hailey's conception is eminent, as well as her dad's death. A crucial decision to move from Houston to Louisiana where the paranormal hub is larger than anywhere else was made in hopes that the covens records would prove helpful in my relentless search. After considerable effort and a long three months, I finally managed to convince Kat to move her and Hailey here as well.

Seated at a desk across the room, my attention is focused

on J, his nimble fingers deftly manipulating the controls of the monitors displaying the feed from the cameras he meticulously installed in the rent house that will soon be Kat and Hailey's new home. Every adjustment, every tweak is executed with precision, the meticulous calibration ensuring there are no shadows left un-illuminated, no corners cast into darkness. The monitors reflect a tapestry of views, each a piece of a puzzle that, when assembled, will provide a safe haven for the girls upon their arrival.

"How are we looking?"

"Good. I've had Xavier, Ryan and Belinda put similar wards on the house that were on the safe house, with an extra shot of 'don't catch on fire' thrown in there."

If it was anyone else, I would tell him it's too soon to joke about the close call, but J thrives off his own dark humor so I let it slide.

"Good. And the cameras?"

"All is good on that front too Boss. We've got exterior views of all areas around the house including street view and neighbors both beside and behind. Then we've got interior views of common areas inside and views of any entry point, window and door. Do you want me to show you how to work it? I'm going to be out of town for the weekend, me and the wife are going to have a baby moon before she gets too uncomfortably pregnant. So I can show you how everything works, and where the controls are so you can operate it in my absence."

"Yea, please."

My attention remains riveted to J as he skillfully maneuvers through the array of monitors, his practiced fingers tapping and scrolling with an effortless grace. With the patience of a saint, J takes the time to guide me through the mechanics of the surveillance system. His explanations are clear and concise, unraveling the intricacies of each function as he demonstrates how to zoom in on a specific area, tilt and pan the camera for a broader view, and adjust the notification settings and sensitivity levels. David, our dedicated head of security, has agreed to stay in Louisiana until we settle all of this. While we wait for the girls impending arrival today, he is busying himself meticulously placing window and glace break sensors along with any other last minute details in their new home. J is a lot more technology savvy than me, and in David's absence, I'm glad to have had him here both to give David a hand in setting all of this up, and to show me how to use it.

"What are the weak points?"

"Well, obviously if either of them leave the house, they are exposed. Then natural exposures like if they are standing in front of a window, or open door. We've installed bullet proof glass on all of the windows with a reflective coating on the outside, so its impossible to see inside during the day. However, at night, they need to keep the curtains drawn, otherwise you can see in. The wards will keep their powers hidden, and unwanted visitors out, but everything has it's limits, you know that."

I know too well just how limited things can be. The events of April serve as a stark reminder of how crucial it is to consider every conceivable angle. I was so focused on keep magical beings out, that I overlooked the potential vulnerabilities posed by humans, like setting a house on fire. Lesson learned though, and luckily we are all alive to learn from it.

"Any luck on the men that took Hailey?"

"No, no luck. None of our medical systems or any of the other covens warlocks have reported subordinates coming in with the injuries that were inflicted. They must have cleaned themselves up and are staying under ground. Are you positive that they are from this time anyway? It would make a lot more sense if they went back through the barrier when it opened and dealt with everything there."

"Hailey was sure of what she said. She was one hundred and ten percent sure that they are from here in this time, they told her so themselves."

"They could have just told her that to throw her off though."

"Yea. But why lie? It's not like we can get to them for another 9 months anyway. What good would it do to tell her they are from this time, where we could actively track them, if they weren't?"

"I guess. But things just done add up. Why would Kat think that they were being chased or wanted them dead if they didn't?"

He's asking all of the questions I've asked myself a million times over, and some that I've asked Kat as well. At minimum the guy that I cut across the face needed stitches, and the other one probably needed is nose reset, maybe even a chipped tooth or two fixed.

The revelation I've been grasping for, the elusive piece of the puzzle that's been just beyond my mental reach, suddenly hits me with an unexpected force. Darting into the kitchen, my fingers instinctively locate a notepad tucked away in the junk drawer. Rifling through its pages, I uncover the notes I scribbled down during my conversation with Kat where she had painstakingly explained what each of the men looked like with the intention to have J look into it. However, with the chaos of our return I threw it into a box as I packed up my home and into this drawer once I moved, completely forgetting about it. Finding it and flipping through a few pages, I find what I wrote down that day. The descriptions are there, fragmented sentences capturing details that I pray will finally give us the lead we've been looking for.

*#1- white. Black eyes. short. Maybe 5'9". Teleport?*

*#2-white. Black eyes. tattoo on neck and head.*

*#3- white. Back eyes. Eye patch with large scar across face.*

*#4-white. Black eyes. red/orange hair. Teeth shaved to points. Crooked nose.*

Shit. I can't believe I didn't see this before now.

"Yo man, what's up? You look freaked."

"Look at this... I wrote all of this down when we were still in Miami."

Handing the notebook to J, I scan his face waiting for a response. As he reads over it a second time, his facial features linger in a state of confusion and I know that I'm going to have to spell it out for him.

"What are the odds that Hailey is right? What if these guys really are from our time? Think about it. I hit one of the guys hard enough that I guarantee he would have needed his nose reset. And the other one, I sliced across his face and he'd be lucky if he didn't lose his eye. What if the guys were wearing masks because they knew we would be able to identify them.

That I would be able to. Hailey said she over heard them say "he's going to kill us" and that they needed to be gone by the time that "he" showed up. What if that 'he' is me? What if I know these guys, and that nights actions are how they got the injuries that Kat recalled them having in the future?"

"I mean, it's a far stretch Boss, and I will be the first to admit I don't know a lot about how time travel works, but I would say it's plausible. Some people think that destiny is predetermined. Maybe things are playing out the way they are supposed to in order to make it back to the night the skipped time."

"I think we need to look into it. It's worth a shot and may be the pebble that we need to get the avalanche rolling. Add black hair to the first ones description, Hailey remembers seeing a black beard before he pulled his mask back down and left."

Tossing J a pen, he writes down what I said and begins to click the top in and out as he thinks.

"You think that if we find these men, it will lead us to Hailey's mom or dad?"

"It's a lead at least. Hailey said that they claimed to be protecting her. Maybe they are protecting one, or both, of her parents too. Look, I know you said you're out of town for the weekend. But would you mind putting these descriptions out through your unofficial channels before you head out? Maybe that will give it some time to stir things up and start getting some tips in, and we can hit the road running when you get back Monday."

"Yea, of course. Hey, we still on for next weekend?"

"Ah, yea. I'll swing by Friday morning and pick the ring

up from you. The reservations at Ruth's are set for seven that evening. Remember though—"

"Yea I know, stay out of sight until she says yes and get it on video."

"You're awesome man, thanks. Best man coming in clutch even before the wedding!"

"Ha! Wait to thank me until after we check out how good the video footage comes out. You tell Kat or Hailey yet?"

"...No, not yet. She knows about them, she hears me talk about them all the time. And I'll tell them soon, there's just never been a good time. Maybe I'll do it this weekend after we get them settled in."

"Hm, well good luck with that. I'm out. I'll send off all of this once I get back to my house, and I'll touch base with you when I get back Sunday or Monday."

With a friendly slap on J's back, I walk him to the door, exchanging a last grin before I turn the lock behind him. Glancing at my watch, I've got roughly two hours before the girls are due to arrive. Wanting to make the best of my time, I snatch up my car keys and head to the store. The least I can do is fill their refrigerator and pantry for them with some of their favorites.

As I navigate the store's aisles, my cart steadily fills with an array of items; ingredients for home-cooked meals, their favorite snacks, and even a bouquet of fresh flowers to add a welcoming touch. A little over four hundred dollars and an hour in a half later, I'm leaving the store and headed towards their house hoping that I beat them there. I'm pulling into their driveway with the bags of groceries nestled securely in my trunk and I can see that luck is on my side, I've managed to beat the girls here. Unlocking the side door I begin to carry armfuls of bags into the house, unpacking each of them with swift efficiency. I begin to slot cans and boxes onto shelves, arrange fresh produce in the refrigerator, and make sure their favorite snacks are readily accessible. Midway through arranging a gallon of Red Diamond sweet tea in the refrigerator, a familiar ding chimes from my pocket. Retrieving my phone, a notification from the security system lights up the home screen notifying me of a car in the driveway. Only having dried foods left to put up, I close the refrigerator and head outside to meet them.

"Welcome to the swamp ladies! Was the drive okay?"

"Yea, we hit some traffic coming out of Houston on I-10 and again coming through Beaumont, but for the most part it was a smooth drive after that. It's not a drive I want to have to make again any time soon though."

"Well, Aunt Kat, maybe if you had let me practice driving you wouldn't mind the drive so much! Where is everyone? I thought you said some of you're guys would be here."

"I'm not sure having a brand new student driver behind the wheel for five plus hours would make the drive any less stressful for your aunt Hailey. The guys are around, David just finished up the security not long before I got here, and J is taking the weekend off but will be back around sometime Monday. I figured y'all might like to get settled before having them around. Plus some of the furniture we ordered won't be here until tomorrow, so it's a little bare in there. Don't worry though, your beds made it in time"

"Thanks Sam, we really appreciate everything that you have done for us."

Kat's gratitude touches me, and I can sense a hint of skepticism in Hailey's demeanor, but I'm optimistic that with time it will all work out. As Kat unlocks the trunk, the latch gives way with a satisfying click, and she begins the process of unloading their belongings. Hailey and I follow suit grabbing bags and boxes that are shoved in the back seat. I told them to only bring the necessities, and that we would buy anything else that they needed once they settled in. However, peering in the overflowing car it's clear that their definition of necessity is different than mine. The vehicle's interior is a puzzle of packages, skillfully arranged like a game of Tetris. Bags are crammed into every conceivable nook, and looking at the trunk, I can't help but wonder how they managed to secure the it shut.

"Did y'all bring enough stuff?"

Kat gives me her oh so famous death glare, and Hailey side eyes the hell out of me, but neither say a word and start walking towards the house, arms full.

"Alright, no jokes, got it."

Following closely behind them, I shoulder the load of bags and boxes that I've gathered, carefully balancing it as I make my way into the house. None of the boxes or bags have any markings on them indicating who they belong to, or what area of the house they go in. Instead of taking the time to sort through the unmarked containers, I opt to leave it in a pile in on the floor in the center of the living room. Coming back in with my second batch of belongings, I take note he girls have taken it upon themselves to start sorting through the initial heap.

Over the course of the next forty-five minutes, I manage

to successfully unload the car, and by the time that I'm done, the girls have made a sizable dent in the pile on the living room floor. Leaving them to do their thing, I decide to focus on finishing the grocery organization that I had begun earlier. It doesn't take long to stock the pantry, and by the time that I'm done, I am exhausted. I can only imagine how Hailey and Kat feel. My original plan was to cook some spaghetti for them, but I opt to order a pizza for delivery instead. Remembering their favorites, I place an order for a half Hawaiian, half supreme pizza.

As I make my way down the hallway, I cross paths with Kat emerging from the primary bedroom and ask if they need any help. She walks back to the living room and begins to sort out three bags and a box from the assortment that had been strewn across the room.

"One bag is towels, you can split them between my bathroom and Hailey's. The box is cleaning supplies and laundry stuff. If you could put all of that up under the sink and in the laundry room that would be great. The other two bags are sheets, pillows, comforters and that kind of think. Hailey's are purple, mine are white. If you could separate those it would be a big help."

Without waiting for me to reply, she picks up another bag and walks back down the hall. Taking this as my cue to get going, I grab the bag of towels and head towards the spare bathroom.

I've finished the towels, bedding, and have just started putting away the cleaning supplies when the chiming of my phone alerts me to the delivery car that is pulling up in front of the house.

"Pizza is here!"

Yelling loud enough for Kat and Hailey to hear me, I stride toward the front door and swing it open, my eyes scanning the front walk for the pizza delivery driver. As he approaches, he begins extracting the pizza box from his red and blue insulated bag, and Hailey is right behind me ready to take it out of his hands. Looking as if she wants to devour the entire thing herself, I wonder if I should have bought two. I scribble my signature on the receipt the driver presents, offering him a nod of thanks before gently shutting the door behind me.

"Is one going to be enough for the two of you?"

"You're not eating with us?"

Hailey's anticipation is palpable as she flips open the pizza box, her eyes widening in sheer delight at the sight of her favorite pizza. Without a moment's hesitation, she reaches in and plucks out a slice, forgoing a paper towel or plate. Meanwhile, as Hailey indulges in her first bite, Kat gracefully makes her way down the hallway, rolling her eyes as Hailey lets out a guttural moan.

"You just couldn't wait, could you Hailey?"

"Sorry Aunt Kat, hot pizza waits for no one."

"All right guys, I've got some stuff I need to take care of back at my place. It looks like you guys have everything handled here though, so I'm going to go head and take off. The alarm panel is by the front door, and there is a second one in the primary suite. I've texted both of you the codes. Please don't forget to set it when y'all shut down for the night and keep the doors locked at all times, even if you are home."

Standing amid the unpacked boxes and half-eaten pizza, I take a moment to reiterate the importance of the security measures I've put in place. I point out each camera, both indoors and outdoors, emphasizing their coverage. Finishing my spiel on security, I'm content that they understand as Hailey rebuttals with a 'we know... we know...' and spews all of the information that I've attempted to drill into their heads back at me. With a quick glance at my keys resting on the kitchen counter, I decide it's time to leave. Locking the door behind me, I make my way to my car, and the engine purrs to life as I settle into the driver's seat. I shoot a text off before putting the car in reverse and slowly back it out of the driveway, avoiding Kat's car next to me, and head home to my girl.

# 16

# Hailey

The weekend has flown by, and as I carefully unpack the last of my belongings, arranging them thoughtfully in my new room, I spend time reminiscing about the few sentimental items that I still have. Among the items that I uncover from the box, a purple ribbon catches my eye, and memories flood my mind. The color matched the dress I wore that special day, a detail that I can't help but smile at. My excitement as a child barely contained itself as my mom tried to tie the ribbon in my hair. As I tenderly tie it in a bow around the post of my bed, I run my fingers down its long silky strand, and close my eyes, letting my mind drift back to that day. I can almost feel my mom's hands gently fumbling with the ribbon, her laughter dancing through the air as I squirmed in anticipation. It is the only thing that I have left from our life before.

Walking back to the box, I pull out a small purple blanket that holds a story of its own. It's the first thing that my aunt bought me after we arrived here. She told me that it was a magic blanket and any time I felt scared, I could put it over my head and become invisible. Toting it around everywhere, the blanket became a shield of comfort, creating security with a promise of invisibility whenever I needed it. Placing it at the foot of my bed, I smooth out the wrinkles so that it lays just right.

Finally, I retrieve a black book, its weight in my hands a testament to the memories it holds and I find myself pausing before looking in it. Taking a deep breath and opening the cover, I stare at a picture of my five year old self. The story behind the picture is one of hope and resilience, a promise my aunt made to create memories in lieu of physical presence. When we first arrived here, I was insistent that I would see my mom again one day, and was so worried that she would miss me growing up. So when my aunt and I went to the store and she bought the blanket, she also picked up a disposable camera. She promised me that we would take a picture any time we did anything fun that I would want to tell my mom about. She ended up taking one right there in the middle of Walmart to prove her point. The picture that stares back at me shows all of the cuts and upcoming bruises that had begun to form, yet I was smiling from ear to ear with pure joy that we had a plan. The book became a series of snapshots, each encapsulating a fragment of our journey together, from the mundane to the extraordinary. As I got older, the pictures became less frequent as I conceded to the fact that my mom was dead and I would never see her again. Yet Aunt Kat insisted that we continue to take them during each birthday trip, insisting that one day I would want these memories.

I gave up hope so long ago that never in a million years did I think that I would actually have the chance of showing them to my mom. I hug the book close to my chest as realization washes over me. I will finally have the chance to share these pictures, these memories, with the very person I believed was forever lost to me.

A knock on my door has me dashing to hide the book between my mattress and box spring. The book itself isn't a secret, but I haven't told my aunt that I heard Sam and her talking, or that I know that we are in a time where my parents are alive. I don't want her to see me looking at it and it raise any red flags, and I need it to stay in a safe spot.

"Yea?"

My aunt opens the door and steps inside as I reach for the now empty box and sit on my bed while I break it down flat.

"You just about done unpacking?"

"Yep. This box was the last one. What about you?"

"I've got a few more things, but I'm almost done too. Sam called a little bit ago and asked if we wanted to eat together tonight. He said he could bring his small pit over, and he could grill some steaks. I told him that I would run it past you first, but I figured it would be nice to have some company after a quiet weekend."

"Yea that sounds good."

"Okay, I'll let him know. Also, the school district here is open tomorrow. I figured we could go ahead and take everything up there to get you enrolled for the fall, that way there are no hiccups later."

"Yea. Sure."

"You okay kid, you seem kind of down."

"I don't know. I'm just not feeling well. New town, Sam isn't as close as he used to be. I guess I'm just worried something is going to happen and we'll be on our own, you know?"

"Hey, you don't need to be worried about stuff like that okay? Let the adults worry about it. Sam and his men have this house wired and maxed out with security measures. And plus, he's only five minutes down the road. We'll be fine, I promise."

"Yea, you're probably right. I'm going to finish hanging up my clothes and then I'll be done. What time is Sam coming over?"

"He was going to go by the store first and grab some stuff, maybe another thirty minutes or so?"

I nod my head in acknowledgment, a gesture that my aunt catches as she turns to leave as she turns to leave, letting me know that she'll be in the kitchen arranging the cabinets if I need anything. I watch her figure move away, her footsteps echoing down the hallway. Yet, even as she departs, an inexplicable sensation begins to gnaw at me. I stare towards my closet knowing that I need to hang up the last of my clothes, but something doesn't feel right. It's a subtle unease, a nagging feeling that resists definition. , but deep in the pit of my stomach something is turning. Foregoing the clothes, I lay back on my bed, phone in hand, and decide to distract myself by browsing social media and listening to music on Pandora.

"Animals" by Dr. Dre has just started playing when I hear Sam's booming voice fill the house. The growing unease that has been plaguing me since I woke up this morning begins to wane. Something about Sam has always calmed me, and given me a feeling of safe, home. The music comes to an abrupt halt as I press pause on my phone. Rising from the bed, I navigate my way to the living room, only to walk in mid argument of Sam and my aunt going back and forth on who will cook the potatoes.

"I've already preheated the oven, just let me do it."

"Kat, you can't even cook bacon! Do you really think that we should trust you to cook a staple component to our meal?"

"That wasn't my fault! Those damn smoke detectors were just sensitive!"

"Do you even know how to cook a potato?"

"Of course I do! You wash it, put it on the rack, and wait until a fork can poke it."

"A little help here Hailey... Please I beg you."

"Sorry, Aunt Kat. I'm on Sam's side, let him cook the potatoes. Do you remember the time you tried to spaghetti and forgot about it? The water boiled out and the noodles literally baked themselves to the bottom of the pot."

"That doesn't count, I got dist— Ugh, you know what forget it. You want to cook the potatoes, be my guest."

Aunt Kat throws up her hands exasperated, and Sam winks at me before walking over to the sink with the grocery bags he carried in.

"Want to give me a hand kid?"

"Oh she can help, but I can't? You guys are ridiculous!"

Sam's hearty laughter mingles with mine as we watch my aunt stomp off to the couch, accompanied by the familiar hum of the television. With a glance and a grin, Sam instructs me to wash the potatoes and then use a fork to poke holes in them, his voice resonating with a mix of patience and practicality. As I begin washing the potatos, he opens up the package of steaks, revealing their marbled texture and rich hues before grabbing seasonings from the bags. Poking holes in the potatoes, their skin gives easily to the gentle pressure and I watch Sam carefully as he makes a liquid concoction of sorts and lays the steaks in it, trying to learn from him as he goes. As I complete my part in preparing the potatoes, Sam motions for me to take over. Handing me a bottle of olive oil and a shaker of salt, my hands follow his lead, coating the potatoes with the smooth sheen of oil and dusting them with the promise of flavor.

"Potatoes take longer than steaks to cook, so we'll let them get started while the steaks marinate for a little bit."

Once I've finished salting the potatoes, Sam helps me put them in the oven, straight on the rack. Grabbing some aluminum foil, he places it on the bottom rack, and explains that it is to catch any drippings from the potatoes. Closing the oven, we walk outside and I help him warm up the grill.

"Your aunt tells me that you might be a little anxious about the new place?"

"I don't know."

"Talk to me kid. You've never been the type to hold back how you're feeling. What's going on?"

It strikes me just how ironic that statement is. I get where he's coming from, I do tell him a lot, and he's both watched me clap back at others and been on the receiving end of it when necessary. But man, if only he knew just how much I hold back.

"I've just got this feeling that I can't seem to shake. I don't know how to explain it."

"Do you think you would feel better if one of my guys came and stayed?"

"Maybe, I mean, I feel a little better with you here."

"Okay, I can arrange for that. I'll have David come by tonight. Your aunt met him back in Florida, so he's not a complete stranger, and J will be back to work tomorrow, so you can meet him then. The three of us can plan a rotation of who stays with y'all until you are comfortable. How does that sound?"

"Sure, we can try it."

Sam brings me in for a hug before wrapping his arms around my head to give me his signature noogie, something he has done since I was a child. If his goal was to lighten the mood, he succeeded as I try to dip out of its way and race towards the back door laughing, Sam in tow.

"It's about time someone gets her to smile."

"What can I say Kat, I'm just awesome like that."

Amid the lighthearted exchange between Sam and my aunt, their playful banter forms a backdrop of familiarity that never fails to warm my heart. Their teasing words and laughter melding with my own. As the aroma of grilling steaks wafts through the air, I help Sam grab the bowls the marinating meat is sitting in and head back outside to put them on the grill.

Between the size of the potatoes and steaks, my aunt and I end up splitting one each, while Sam loads his plate to the brim. Not all of our furniture has been delivered yet, so in the absence of a proper table, the living room transforms into our dining space, with the couch providing a comfortable backrest as we sit cross-legged on the floor. My aunt joins me, balancing her plate and drink as she settles in, with Sam right behind her. Just as Sam is about to sit down, the ringtone of his phone pierces through the air. Grabbing his plate from his hand so that he can answer it, I listen in on his side of the conversation.

"Hey, what's up? Oh cool, yea, no I'm over here at Kat and Hailey's house. I just got finished grilling and have extras if you're in the mood for steak and baked potatoes. Yeah, okay cool, see you in a few."

Hanging up the phone, he puts it back in his pocket and sits down. Grabbing his plate back from me he digs in without saying a word while me and my aunt stare at him, then each other.

"So, I guess David is coming over now?"

Sam looks at me with a mouth full, confused, before his brain gets with the program and recognition strikes.

"Oh, no. That was J. He got back in town a little early and wanted to drop by to introduce himself. I hope that's okay. I figured you guys could meet him now, so it is a little less awkward when he stays tomorrow."

"Wait, who's staying here and why?"

Sam and I both look at each other and realize that while we talked about a game plan, neither of us keyed my aunt in on what it was. Luckily Sam picks up the slack and fills her in taking the blame.

"Ah, sorry. Hailey and I were talking outside, and I just feel like until you guys get settled in, it might be nice to have some extra security around the house. You've already met David. I've talked to him and he'll be here tonight. J was supposed to come by tomorrow and introduce himself and switch off shifts, but he's going to come by tonight to say hi and chat for a bit, then will be back tomorrow."

I can see it in my aunts face that she's going to disagree, a subtle tension in her features telling me that she might voice her reservations. I want to stop her before she does and ask why, my words hang in the air as Sam's phone dings diverting my attention. Simultaneously the exterior lights cast fleeting shadows on the walls, suggesting the arrival of J. Not wanting to seem too eager, I stay seated as Sam gets up and walks towards the front door. Not counting the guys who took me, this will be the first paranormal besides Sam and my aunt that I've met, and I am exploding with excitement and curiosity on the inside. I listen as a car door shuts and Sam opens the front door, and then hear the same familiar voice that filled Sam's car every hour, on the hour in Key West.

"Hey Boss! I can smell the steaks from here!"

"Weigle, my man. If you think they smell good just wait until you taste them."

# 17

# Hailey

My head whips around with such force that it almost sends my plate and cup tumbling to the floor. Standing in the doorway facing Sam is the last person that I ever expected to see. Startled, I scramble to my feet, my heart racing in tandem with the flurry of thoughts racing through my mind. Looking back at my aunt to make sure that I'm not hallucinating, and see that her shock mirrors mine, her face white as a ghost. Slowly, hesitantly, I pivot my attention back to the doorway and watch as the two men embrace each other in some weird rendition of a bro hug before Sam leads him into the house, locking the door behind them.

"Hey man, this is Kat and that's Hailey. Kat, Hailey, this is—"

"John."

Sam looks at me bewildered, as if I have five heads

when I finish his sentence. His gaze shifting between me and my aunt.

"Yea... How did you— Kat are you okay, you don't look so good."

"Actually, yea I don't feel so good. If you'll excuse me."

The three of us watch as my aunt gets up and fast walks down the hall before slamming the door to her room closed.

"You're John Weigle."

"Hailey, how do you know that?"

I can tell by the way that Sam is standing, and the levelness of his voice that he's trying to remain calm. That makes one of us, because right now, I am freaking out.

"You know my dad."

They are the only words that I seem to be able to muster up, but they get my point across. Sam looks from me to John, and back to me. By the look on John's face, he has no idea what he just walked in on.

"Hailey, what are you talking about? How would John know your dad?"

"He is my dad's best friend. I grew up with him telling me stories of all of the things that him and my dad did together. Like the time that they went skiing in Utah, and my dad's ski got stuck on the lift, so when he went to get off, he face planted into the snow. Or the time that they were paint balling, and John went to tap out because he got shot by someone, and as he removed his mask my dad accidentally shot him in the forehead so he had a lump in the middle of his head that was bruised for weeks, and my dad kept calling him a unicorn. Johns son was my best friend."

I'm not sure who's paler at this point, John or Sam, but

neither of them are talking. Instead, both of them are standing there, slack-jawed and staring at me.

"Are you okay Sam? You look about like Aunt Kat right now."

"Yea, no, I'm fine. I just need to sit down for a minute."

John follows Sam into the living room, and as they settle onto the couches, a whirlwind of thoughts race through my mind. My gaze briefly falls upon the remnants of our meal, temporarily forgotten on the floor. I quickly gather the plates and utensils, placing them on the counters in the kitchen, almost on autopilot and rejoin them on the couches. The energy in the room seems to shift, my initial shock beginning to give way to an undercurrent of excitement.

"Sam, don't you see what this means. This means that we can find my parents, we can save my mom, maybe even my dad too. I mean, your best friend hasn't died yet, right John? Oh! That must mean that you know my mom too!"

"No, he uh, he's still alive. He just, um... Oh God."

"Hailey... I don't think you understand. Shit. I don't know how I didn't see this. Hailey, John can't be your dads best friend... "

Sam's words don't even register to my ears before I instantly begin to dismiss how.

"Of course he is! They were best friends for years before he died. John told me so himself."

"Hailey, that would mean that I'm your dad."

Sam's statement is said just an octave above a whisper, his facial expression a mixture of defeat and pain. Why won't he listen to me? Why is he ignoring what I'm saying?

"What? No! That's not possible."

"Hailey, those stories that you just shared, those are about me. Those are things that I did."

" But no, that can't be, my dads name was—"

"Theodore."

Sam and I say the name at the same time, and it's my turn to be quiet now as the implications of this settle in. None of this makes sense. How could Sam be my dad?

"I don't understand."

"My first name is Theodore, but so was my dads. So as I kid, I went by my middle name, Samuel. All of my friends called me Sam. After my dad passed, the name just kind of stuck, and I've continued to go by that. Hardly anyone knows my real name."

My heart races within my chest, the rhythm echoing the flurry of emotions that surge through me. I can't believe what is happening right now, It's as if the fabric of reality has shifted, revealing a long-concealed truth. I've spent my entire life missing a part of me, that was actually right in front of me for the past eight years. Shocked, happy, excited, I'm not sure there is a word for how I feel right now. So instead of searching for a word, I let my gaze linger over Sam, it's as if I'm seeing him with new eyes. The features I've come to know over the years, the way his eyes crinkle when he smiles, the set of his jaw when he's deep in thought, take on a new significance.

"John, once told me that I had my dads eyes."

"I've never looked that closely before, but yea, I'd say you do."

It's a powerful realization that a part of my identity, a piece of my past, has been standing beside me all along. Sam, is clearly in as much shock as I am right now, with little to no words as we stare at each other.

With each passing second, the sense of connection intensifies. It's not just in the physical resemblance, though that's certainly striking. It's in the way he carries himself, and the way his laughter rings in the room. The revelation has upended the narrative of my life in a way I could never have foreseen, and It's emotional tsunami leaves me grappling to find my footing amid the swirling currents.

"Hailey, what *is* your moms name? I've heard both you and Kat talk about her, and Kat and I have talked about it being easier to find your dad due to him being a supernatural. But I've never considered that it might be important to know her name until now.

"Sarah, her name was Sarah."

The whistle that comes from John as he shakes his head has me looking over at him and looking back to Sam as he runs his hand over his face. Without having to ask, I already know the answer to the question that sits on the forefront of my mind.

"So you know her, huh?"

"Know her? He's about to ask her to marry him."

John's statement has me reeling in shock, and my fingers curl around the edge of the couch cushion in an attempt to ground myself. The stories John shared always centered around their friendship, their adventures, the escapades that they embarked upon together. No one told met that my parents had been engaged. I mean sure, Aunt Kat has talked about believing that they were in love, but never once did she mention that they had been a ring involved. Briefly I wonder if it's possible that the way things are playing out in time are changing. Maybe this is the first glimmer of hope for a different outcome. Scared to jinx it, I opt to keep my suspicion to myself and listen to the conversation that Sam and John are having.

"I don't know Boss, I've never gotten any other feeling from her than being human. You would think one of us would have sensed or seen something."

"It just doesn't make sense though J, how else would Hailey have as much power as she does? Don't get me wrong, my powers being passed down would still be pretty damn powerful, but it doesn't account for the amplification or the glow of her aura."

"I mean, I can do some more digging, but we did a pretty extensive background check when you decided to start seeing her. I can't imagine how absolutely nothing paranormal came up in her background if she's tied to this world."

"I mean, we missed me being a contender for Hailey's dad, so clearly our methods aren't foolproof. Dig some more and see what you can come up with. Her parents died in her early twenties, maybe start there and branch out."

"Hey, not fair. I told you that you were on that list, just like me and David. But we all agreed that it was safe to take the three of us out of the running."

"I know. I know. Look, just try and see if we might have missed something. David is going to be here any minute and I can rope him in on everything as well. It can give him something focus on tonight. I'll go talk to Sarah and see if she can shed some light on her past while you run down your channels as well. We'll meet here tomorrow morning and see if we can piece together something."

"Does that mean that my mom is close? Can I see her? Where is she?"

Both guys heads jerk towards me, almost like they are surprised that I'm still there or that they had forgotten about me. Sam recovers first after a fight with his jaw deciding if it will stay open or closed.

"Let me talk to your aunt first. I'm not really sure how this whole time travel thing works when you aren't the one with the powers. I know that you can't run into yourself, but I don't know if coming across yourself while someone is pregnant with you counts towards that."

Sam's eyes go wide, his jaw back slack, and I can see the wheels turning behind those piercing blue eyes as his brain catches up to the words coming out of his mouth. It's clear that he is just now putting it together.

"Oh shit."

"Ha, congrats Pops! With that, I'm out. I'll take your advice and run it through my channels. If anything super important pops up I'll text you guys, but if not then I will see you guys in the morning. "

Sam stands and gives John a pat on the back and watches as he walks out of the front door, clearly still shell shocked from his little epiphany. Taking this as an opportunity to grab a drink, I head into the kitchen and refill the cup that I had earlier. Sam is still standing in the middle of the living room, staring off into space when his phone starts chirping.

"You going to check that?"

"Huh? Oh. Yea... Looks like David just got here."

"Do you want me to let him in? Looks like your feet are cemented in place."

"Very funny kid. You should be a comedian some day. No, I'll let him in."

It him takes a moment, but Sam eventually starts to move. Curiosity pulling me forward, I slowly follow behind him, stopping in the living room as he heads towards the door and positioning myself so that I can see who this guy is once the door is open. Leaning against the door frame between the hall and living room proves to give me the angle I'm seeing as the door swings wide. I'm able to catch a sliver of a glimpse of him, before Sam shifts blocking my view, leaving me only to be able to see the guys hand still raised in a half knock.

"Hey David, come on in, I've got a few things to catch you up on before I head out."

"Yea, sure, thanks."

The eerily familiar voice that floats down the entry way has me stopping in my tracks.

"Hey, your—"

My heart lurches as Sam's movement grants me a clearer view of the scene unfolding outside the door. It's as if time slows to a crawl, each detail etched into my mind with razor-sharp clarity. My eyes dart between the man standing just inside the doorway and the figure lurking behind him across the street. My breath catches in my throat as recognition dawns and my voice gives out as I see the man from my hotel room raise his arms in a shooters stance. My world narrows to a singular point as a sharp crack splits the air, the sound of a gunshot echoing with a sickening finality.

"Sam!"

David barrels through the door pushing Sam into the house, and slamming the door closed before spinning in my direction.

"Was anyone hit?"

I shake my head feverishly in response, and my eyes widen in horror as Sam staggers further into the house, his hand clutching at his chest, blood staining his shirt. A wave of panic surges through me as the horrific scene unfolds. My gaze remained fixed on Sam, his face contorting in pain as he leans against the wall for support. A gasp escapes my lips as I register the dark stain blooming on his shirt, a stark contrast against the fabric's pale hue. Slowly lowering himself to his knees his hand leaves a trail of crimson across the wall, and my stomach churns as the reality of the situation crashing down like a ton of bricks. David's swift action breaks through my haze of shock as he rushes to Sam's side, his movements precise and urgent. The intensity in his eyes is palpable as he removes his shirt and bunches it up, pressing it against the wound.

"Look for an exit wound! Hailey! Help me look!"

The rush of David's words and the panic in his voice snap me to attention. Slamming down to my knees I search Sam's back and sides looking for any other sign of blood.

"I don't know,there's blood everywhere. It's hard to see"

David rolls Sam onto his back, and motions for me to lift Sam's head onto my lap. Gently, I position myself, angling my legs so that they support Sam's upper body, while my lap serves as a makeshift pillow. As Sam's head rests on my lap, I focus on his face, my concern growing as I notice the small pool of blood at the corner of his mouth. My breath catches in my throat, and I instinctively look to David, seeking some type of direction or reassurance.

"Help him!"

"Hailey, get my phone out of my pocket and call John back here."

"John? Why aren't we calling 911? He needs help!"

"He's got a better chance with John than with human doctors. Hailey, you have to trust me, call John."

Grabbing David's phone, I hold it up to his face to unlock and frantically search for John's number. The phone doesn't finish ringing a full ring before John's voice comes through the line.

"Hey D, what's up?"

"John, get back here! You have to get back here now!"

"Hailey? Whoa, what's going on?"

"It's Sam, he's been shot. John you have to hurry. There's blood everywhere, and David is trying to stop it, but it's coming out of his mouth too and I don't know what to do."

"Fuck. Okay, yea I'm turning around right now. I'm still in the neighborhood."

John hangs up the phone before I am aware that the conversation is over. I sit there for a second with the phone still to my ear as I try to process everything, the weight of his words settling over me. Life couldn't be this cruel could it? Leaving me orphaned at five, only to give me the gift of my father without telling me, and then take him away as soon as we meet each other. How is that fair? How is any of this fair? My attention snaps back to the immediate crisis as Sam's breathing becomes raddled and the intermittent coughing progresses, leaving specks of blood spattered on the wall next to us. Alarmed, and worried that John won't get here in time, it occurs to me that there is another adult in this house that might be able to help.

"Help! Aunt Kat help!!"

"D, you've got to take her. Take her and keep her safe. Call your guys if you have to. Just don't let anything happen to her."

Sam's voice is strained and labored, his words coming out in short spurts as he attempts to talk. I glance over at David, who remains steadfast by Sam's side and can see that under no circumstances will he be leaving Sam alone, regardless of the orders that he's just been given. While I don't know him, It's in that moment that David gaines a little bit of my respect. Before he can give Sam a refusal, the sudden slam of the back door reverberates through the room, and the noise of it has me whipping my head around to find John rushing in.

"What happened?"

"It was the guy, the one from my hotel room. When Sam opened the door for David, he was standing across the street. I heard a gun go off, and then David pushed Sam in the house and closed the door. It wasn't until after we were all inside that we noticed that Sam had been shot, we looked for an exit wound but couldn't find one. His breathing, it sounds funny now and he's coughing up blood, and David said to call you instead of 911. He said that you could help him."

Everything comes out in a single breath, and I'm looking between Sam and John expecting I don't know what, to happen. Some glowing hands, a wand, a magic potion... Anything that will tell me that calling him was the right choice and that he's going to be able to help. Instead, he moves at what seams a snails pace as he lowers himself next to me and moves Sam's head from my lap into his.

"Go D. Take her and go."

The hoarseness of sames voice now comes out as a breath of a whisper.

"He's right, I've got him, y'all go. We don't know where the shooter is, you need to keep her safe."

Just when I think that David is going to argue and put up a fight to stay, he gives a short nod of his head.

"Come on kid, time to go."

Before I can say anything, David hands the wadded up shirt to John, leans down and throws me up and over his shoulder. Learning from my lesson three months ago, I lay still as the familiar feeling of speeding through space takes over and the world streaks by in small spurts.

# 18

# Hailey

"What the hell is your problem? I wasn't done there! I didn't want to leave, we need to go back and help John save him! You can't keep throwing me over your shoulder like a rag doll and just take me wherever you want, when you want! Take me back. Now!"

"I'm sorry Hailey, but we had to leave. Like Sam said, I need to keep you safe."

"Does Sam know who you are? Does he know it was you who took me back in Florida? Because I'm betting if he did, we wouldn't be having this conversation, would we? No, if he knew who you were, you wouldn't be allowed anywhere near me!"

"Speaking of, how do you know who I am?"

His question gives me pause, but I recover quickly.

"Your voice. A girl isn't likely to forget the voice of someone who kidnapped her."

I can tell that he's thinking it over, along with his next step as he chews on the inside of his cheek. Meanwhile, my frustration simmers beneath the surface, a potent mix of anger and anxiety. Furious, that he took me again, and anxious to get back to Sam and John, fuels my impatience and I contemplate throwing a fit. It wouldn't exactly scream mature teenager, or be very becoming of me, but I'm willing to do whatever it takes to ensure that I'm back with Sam. And right now, I just need to know Sam is alive. My gaze sweeps around the room, scanning for anything I could potentially use as a distraction or a means of escape.

"Look kid, how about we make a deal. Let me make sure that we weren't followed and that our location is secure, then I'll call John and see how things are on there end. Good?"

Not even close, but it's going to have to do until I can get out and track my own way back. I nod my head in agreement, an outward appear to engage in David's activities, while my mind is already racing ahead, concocting a strategy for escape. David starts moving around the mostly empty house, checking window, shutting blinds, and occasionally looking at his phone. My eyes trail him as he performs his tasks, pretending to show interest in his progress. My thoughts jump from one possibility to another. The back door that we came through is in front of me, with another door off of the kitchen. A garage, laundry room, or pantry are my top guesses, but without being sure I decide the risk wouldn't be worth it. There's nothing like making a run for it only to trap yourself in a closet. Continuing to watch him, the living room's six windows serve as potential exit points, and briefly I fantasize about busting through one or sneaking out of it. If

I've learned anything in the last few months though, it's that Sam doesn't take security lightly. If this house is anything like the safe house, our new house here, or even like what he did to our Houston house after we got back from Florida, between the wards and alarms I won't make it far. Pivoting around now, there's a study of some sort that's open to the living room and next to it is the entry way and front door. My gaze travels around the open floor plan, studying the layout of the house. An angular wall catches my attention, revealing closed doors that likely lead to various rooms. I silently curse the modern architectural trend that prioritizes open spaces over traditional walls and divisions. The house's layout reveals itself as both a blessing and a curse, providing me with clear sight lines but few opportunities to disappear unnoticed. As we complete our circuit around the house, my heart sinks and I try my best to hide my disappointment as I realize that my best chances for escape lie at the front or back doors.

"Where is my Aunt? If you aren't going to take me back to Sam, then you can at least go and get her."

"Sorry kid, no can do. My sole job right now is to make sure you stay safe."

"Don't you think my aunt can handle that? I mean she's kept me safe just fine by herself for the past decade."

"Actually, no, I don't. Hailey, think about it. Twice now you've almost died. Once in Florida, and just now. Sam had a solid plan in Florida to keep you safe, yet somehow your location was compromised. That's not even bringing up the fact that Sam had your house here under complete lock down. There were five people who knew about it. Sam, John, me, you, and your aunt. That's it Hailey. Yet somehow the same guy from Florida found you within a day of you being here. We've got a mole somewhere, and we can't trust anyone."

"Three times actually. I almost died three times. You're forgetting when you set a house on fire with me in it, and it nearly burnt to the ground."

"I had good intentions, and you didn't almost die then. I got you out just fine, you didn't have a singed hair on your head."

"Yea? And if Sam or my aunt hadn't of made it out, what then? What if they had been asleep and died of smoke inhalation before they ever made it outside? Sam wouldn't have been able to lower the wards to break the window, and we would have all died."

"Yea, well it wouldn't be the first mistake that's been made."

"What's that supposed to mean?"

David rubs his face in the same way that Sam does when he's frustrated, and I can't help but wonder if this is a tick that they've picked up from each other, or if it's just a coincidence.

"Hailey, I need to know what you know. Start to finish give me every detail regardless of how small it is. Even if your not sure it's something that actually happened or if you think you dreamed it, I need to know."

It's an odd request, but it's not the first time that someone has asked me something similar. It's abundantly clear that David isn't going to budge on the whole 'keep you safe if it's the last thing I do' thing, and I know I need to bide my time. Maybe if I wait him out, he'll fall asleep and I can try to get out then.

"Check on Sam first, then I'll tell you."

Aiming his sigh at me, David pulls out his phone. The call rings all the way through before dumping into John's voicemail.

"They didn't answer, now talk."

"No, call Sam's phone." Giving me more of a growl than a sigh this time, David obliges. The phone rings three times before John's voice comes across the speaker phone.

"Y'all safe?"

"Yea, how's—"

The line goes dead. David's face scrunches inward, just as baffled at the abrupt ending of the phone call as I am.

"He's probably busy. He'll call back when he gets a minute, now talk"

Taking a deep breath, I begin recounting my story as David has instructed. My words flow like a river, carrying with them memories and emotions that I've held onto for years. I start at the very beginning, describing the night they broke into our house. My hands move as I talk, gesturing to illustrate how I hid or ran, trying to capture the essence of my experiences. With every detail, I aim to provide a vivid picture of my life. Moving around as a small kid, our decision to settle in Houston, the routines and mundane moments that formed our days. I recount the annual birthday trips with Aunt Kat, the laughter, the joy, and all of the fine details that fall in between. As I delve deeper into my story, I recall the emotions that accompanied each event. The fear, the frustration, the determination, the hope. I speak with honesty, letting the rawness of my experiences shine through. I describe the moments of doubt and the fears that I hid deep within. I try not to leave anything out, but being put on the spot doesn't always lead to the most accurate account of thing. Satisfied that I've at least hit the big things my voice wavers as I come to the events of tonight, describing the shocking revelations that unfolded in front of my eyes. I recount how the familiar face of John rocked my world, how the past and the present collided in a maelstrom of emotions. I detail the arrival of the assailant, the gunshot, and the chaos that followed. My voice trembles as I recount Sam's injuries, the blood, the desperation, and the overwhelming fear. I conclude my narrative, feeling a mix of relief and vulnerability. I look to David, my eyes searching his face for any sign of understanding or reaction, hoping that my words have conveyed the complexity of my life and the urgency of our situation.

"Why didn't you just tell Sam about everything? I don't understand why you kept it all a secret."

"There are a lot of things you don't understand Hailey. I couldn't tell Sam because if I did, there was a good chance that he would have done something different and it would have altered the time line. Even the smallest change in decision could have a ripple effect down the road. The fact that he knows he's your dad... I don't know how that's going to affect things..."

"How do I know that I can trust you? You say there's a mole, how do I know it's not you?"

"You heard Sam. He told me to keep you safe, so clearly he trusts me. I need you to do the same."

"Yea, well he trusted me with my aunt this whole time, and now your telling me maybe we shouldn't trust her. Seems a little ironic, don't you think?"

David huffs at me before turning towards the front of

the house, looking at his phone again, and I know that our conversation isn't going to be productive. Giving up, I walk over to the first door to peek inside in search of a bed, and instead find an empty room. Doing the same and opening the other doors, I find two more empty rooms and a bathroom. Resolving to having no bed to sleep on, I make my way to the love seat, laying across it and making myself comfortable. If David wants any sleep, he can take the recliner.

***

I'm not sure how long I've slept when I'm woken up to hushed whispers. Lifting my head up just enough to peer over the arm rest on the other side, I see David talking with a very concerned looking John.

"I need to go and tell her D, and I need you to come with me. I know you don't want to leave the kid, so Kat is on her way here."

"I'm not leaving her with Kat, John. It's all playing out again and for all I know she's in on it."

"Then she can stay in the car or something. We'll figure it out, but we need to do this together."

"What's going on? John? Where's Sam?"

As both John and David turn their attention toward me, a weighty silence settles over the room, punctuated only by the soft sound of their footsteps as they approach. My heart races in anticipation, the tension in the air almost palpable. I expect John to be the one to answer me, but instead it's David who squats down eye level to me. My gaze shifts between David and John, and in that moment, I notice the telltale signs of grief etched in John's eyes. The reddened rims, the shadows of recent tears and in that moment I know the news isn't going to be good. My throat tightens, and I feel the words I want to speak catch. It's as if the floodgates of my feelings have opened, and my mind is overwhelmed with a rush of fear, confusion, and sadness. I try to swallow past the lump forming in my throat, but it's a struggle to do so. My breath hitches, and I can feel the tears gathering behind my eyes, blurring my vision. David's presence in front of me is a mix of compassion and gravity. His eyes, full of understanding and empathy, hold mine for a moment, while I brace myself for what's to come.

"Hailey, do you remember what I said earlier when I mentioned that it wouldn't be the first time a mistake had been made?

As David meets my eyes and leans in slightly, his expression is soft yet laden with the gravity of the situation, and I find myself revisiting our earlier conversation. I nod my head yes still unable to speak in fear that the swell of tears that have built in my eyes will come crashing down like a wave breaking over a reef. I remember him saying it, and calling him out in it, but now that I really think about it I realize that he never answered me.

"Good, okay. Hailey, do you ever feel moments of dejavu? Like you've seen something before that you know you never have, or been somewhere you know you've never been? Or even that your having a conversation that you've had before, but don't know why it feels so familiar?"

I don't have to think about it to know what he's talking about. As David's words resonate with me, I'm transported back to a series of memories, each carrying the weight of that inexplicable feeling he's addressing. The feeling has overcome me so much that I don't even question it anymore. I vividly recall the time we moved into our house in Houston, and the specific moment I confided in her, describing how I felt like I'd been there before. It was the first time that I had gotten the feeling, and she brushed it off saying it was impossible because we had never been in Texas before. I didn't question her, because like she said, we really never had been to Texas before. It may have been the first time that I had had the feeling, but it certainly wasn't the last. The feeling had a tendency to wash over me at the most unexpected times; walking down a new street, hearing a particular song, even meeting new people. It was like a secret connection to moments I had never lived. Not really sure where David is going with this, I cautiously try to find my voice to answer him.

"Yea?"

A single word is all that I can trust as I speak in the softest voice possible. What was supposed to be a statement comes out as a question dripping in my confusion and hesitation.

"Do you know why?"

My anxious feelings and tears are beginning to fill with rage. I'm quickly becoming tired of the questions with no answers. I don't care that the dam has broken and hot streaked tears are now flowing freely down my cheeks, I just want to know where Sam is.

"Why won't you answer my question? Where is Sam?"

"I did everything that I could Hailey, but Sam is gone. I was able to heal the ribs it fractured and the hole in his lung, but the bullet that went in his side must have damaged his heart. Nothing that I was doing was working, no amount of healing or energy that I was pouring into him was making him better. Then his heart, it just, stopped. I couldn't bring him back."

The room seems to hold its breath as John's emotions spill over. He doesn't try to muffle the choked sounds of sobs that come from him in that last sentence as he grabs at his shirt just above his own heart, and my heart aches for him as the pain in his face matches mine. I spent the first five years of my life listening to the stories of him and my dad. He became a link to a past I never had the chance to experience firsthand, and I know that John would have given anything to have been able to save Sam. Despite the immense pain radiating from John, a strange numbness settles over me. It's not anger or sadness; it's a void. A vacuum that seems to suck away my ability to feel anything in this moment.

"—stuck in a cycle."

Davids words pull me out of my fog, and I want to ask him to repeat himself. Before I can, John interjects.

"D, we really need to go. You can talk more in the car if you need to but we need to go now."

"Where are we going?"

Both men look at me, and I can't tell by their expressions what they are thinking. David looks as if he wants to argue about something, and John stares at me with a pain painted on his face.

"You really do have is eyes you know."

His words hit me like a ton of bricks right in my gut, slicing through my numbness. I can't help but to smile just a little at the sentiment as the waterworks start back up in my eyes.

"So you've told me. Thanks for that."

"Hailey, we have to go tell Sam's next of kin that he passed. I know this might be hard for you, but we can't leave you here. You can come and stay in the car if you want. We'll be a few feet away from you, and John and I will have eyes on the car at all times."

"Yea. Okay, sure."

They aren't giving me much of a choice, so what else can I say? My body moves off of the couch without any conscious thought, and I follow them in a solemn procession. Stepping outside, a heavy silence envelopes us, save for the faint rustling of leaves and the distant hum of a car passing by. The early mornings air is cool against my skin, and a shiver runs down my spine, though it's not entirely due to the temperature. Reality seems to have shifted into an alternate dimension, a world where the unthinkable has become my reality. David heads out first, leaving John and I behind while he checks the perimeter of the house, and the car before motioning us his way. The doors open with a soft click, and I slide into the back seat, the leather cool against my skin. I buckle my seat belt mechanically, my movements automatic. Leaning my head against the window, I close my eyes briefly, the weight of the moment pressing down on me. How can it be that just hours ago I was talking with Sam, and now he's no longer apart of this world. Tears escape, tracing wet paths down my cheeks, but I don't bother to wipe them away, leaving them as a reflection of the turmoil within me.

# 19

# Hailey

As the car comes to a halt, and the engine's soft purr fades into the dawn, I stay seated, not bothering to open my eyes. A voice, I can't discern whose, penetrates the fog in my mind mentioning that they'll be back soon. The sound of car doors opening and closing echoes around me, leaving me in an almost suspended state. The weight of grief, confusion, and disillusionment is suffocating. It's as though my emotions have been drained, and I find it hard to care about anything at this point. My entire life has been a lie. I've lost all of the people that I care about, my mom, Sam, and now possibly even my aunt, if David is right in his assumptions. At this point one can only hope that the gunman from earlier shows up and takes me out of my misery. After all, without them, what's the point in living?

Seconds tick by, turning into what feels like minutes before the sound of anguish and loss rings in my ears, of someone being told their loved one isn't coming back. It hits me then that from what John told me growing up, Sam's dad died when he was a teenager and his mom in his early twenties. I can't remember mention of any brothers or siblings, and I find myself now curious who Sam's next of kin is. With a hesitant resolve, I open my eyes, the world comes into focus freezing me in place as the view of an all familiar house with the sun peeking just over the roof comes into view. David and John are standing on the front steps just under the porch facing away from me and blocking my view of the person they are talking to, but I can see dainty arms wrapped around John. My seat belt is unbuckled, and before I know it, I'm stepping out of the car. The two men turn toward the sound of the door, and their expressions shift from concern to surprise as they lock eyes with me. I follow their gaze to the red oak door in front of us, and the realization crystallizes. This isn't dejavu like David talked about earlier. No, I have been here. Lived here.

"Hailey, you need to stay in the car."

Johns voice carries over to me as I slowly walk up the sidewalk towards the house, ignoring his request.

"Hailey?"

The sweet notes of a Southern voice reach my ears, drawing me into its embrace. My breath catches as sandy brown hair peeks out from behind John, a shade that mirrors my own, and my heart races with a mixture of anticipation and disbelief. The face that comes into view is the face I've found myself trying to remember for years. Her face is flush, her cheeks wet, and her eyes are red as fresh tears continue to fall, but even so I recognize it instantly. Every impulse in me screams to close the gap between us, to rush into my moms arms and bury myself in her embrace.

"Hailey, really, you need to stay in the car. Go back now."

"She's fine John. Lets get inside and I'll warm up some tea for everyone."

The world goes silent in the pause between her words and John's surrender, and I want nothing more than for her to keep talking as I soak in every word she says. The crickets and bullfrogs resume their song as we make our way inside. The living room, with its subtle arrangement of furniture, remains unchanged, inviting a flood of memories to resurface. Curious if the house is the same, I announce that I'm going to use the restroom and without waiting for directions I head down the hall to where it is. Pretending like I don't know where I'm going, I open the first bedroom door on the left and find a queen sized bed with its white headboard and foot board staring back at me. The comforter is different, and it lacks the drawing that I did in permanent marker, but is otherwise utterly the same. Closing the door and moving further down the hall, I make my way to the next room on the right. The scent of her perfume hits me as I open the door and I'm so consumed by its presence, I stall with the door halfway open. Gathering my strength I open it the rest of the way and am met with an unfamiliar messy bed, but the chair in the corner brings me back. The golden oak rocker that used to be in my room is tucked in the corner nearest the wall, and on its back hangs the teal and white afghan that I fondly remember rapping my fingers in as my mom would read me bedtime stories. I know that there is a bathroom through the door on the right, but I opt not to use it. Hanging there for a moment longer taking in her scent, I finally close the door continue on my trek. Skipping what I know to be a linen closet and a jacket closet, I pause before opening the last bedroom door. Grief crashes over me as I'm met with an emptiness that mirrors the void within me and I immediately shut the door unable to process the emotions. Pivoting to the door that sits at the end of the hall, I walk into the restroom and try to get my emotions under control.

Pacing back and forth in the small space proves impossible, and instead I slide down the wall parallel to the sink, holding my head between my hands. The room that was empty, was my room. Void of any belongings, it is a stark reminder that I don't exist in this world, and that my mom has no idea who I am. It's hard not to find the irony in this cruel world. A thought begins to tickle in the back of my mind, and as it comes to fruition, realization sets in. David was so worried about Sam making different choices and affecting the time line that he couldn't even tell him that he was trying to help. With Sam no longer here, what if the events of tonight cause me to no longer exist in this world too? What are the implications to me, if my future self is never born? I pinch myself and pat around, making sure that I haven't somehow become a ghost, or that I'm not slowly fading away like you see in movies. Satisfied that I'm not, I get up and wash my face before returning to the living room, making a mental note to ask my aunt or David how all of this works.

Returning to the living room, I find myself seated at the kitchen table. The rhythmic whistling of the kettle pulls me into a trance, summoning memories of all the times that my mom made hot tea for me. Whether I was sick, sad, happy, needing comfort, celebrating, or really any occasion. My mom was ready with two cups in hand. It started with me stealing sips of hers at breakfast, and morphed into a bonding thing. Eventually she began making me my own cup, albeit not as hot as hers, and we would just sit and talk. I can't believe that I had forgotten about that, about any of this. She sets John and Davids cups in front of them before returning with mine, creamer and some sugar, before grabbing hers and joining the three of us. We sit quietly as we each pour sugar and cream into our cups, the clinking of our spoons against the glass echoing in the room, no one wanting to be the first to talk.

"What happened?"

"Sarah, I don't think—"

"Just tell me John, I need to know."

"He was caught in the crossfire of an altercation outside one of his rent houses. He was shot, and the damage that he incurred was catastrophic. The doctors tried, but they just couldn't save him."

My cup hovers at my mouth and I stop mid blow to give David a questioning look. The story that John just told her isn't what happened at all, but the small shake of Davids head tells me not to question it.

"Sarah, there's something else. Sam gave this to me a few weeks ago to hold on to, and planned to give it to you on Friday. Even though he's not here to go through with his plans, I think that you should still have it."

John reaches into his pocket, pulling out a small black velvet box and hands it over to her. I watch as she opens it with shaking hands, and pulls out a ring that I recognize as the one she used to wear around her neck. I can remember her telling me that it was a ring my dad had given her, but she never told me that it was an engagement ring from a proposal that she never got.

"He loved you Sarah. He wanted to marry you and start a life with you. I'm so sorry that he's not here to tell you himself."

The sobs that come from her are soul shattering, and I find myself crying with her. As David coughs and John clears his throat, I see that both men are also on the brink of tears and trying to stay strong, looking anywhere but her.

"Thank you John. I know you're here to break the news to me, and to console me, but y'all lost him too."

Her words are choked as she says them, but the sincerity in them is palpable. A wave of emotion comes over me as I realize that this is the last gift that she will ever receive from him, and I understand why she never took it off.

"Would anyone like some more tea?"

"No—"

"No—"

"Yes ma'am."

"You really are as sweet as he said you are, aren't you Hailey?"

A soft smile spreads across her face through the tears, and her words catch me off guard.

"He talked about me?"

"Of course he did! He talked about you all of the time. I don't know if he ever told you, but he referred to you as his unofficial daughter."

Now its my turn to choke back a sob. If only she knew. If only he had known. Maybe things would have been different.

"I don't mean to cut things short Sarah, but Hailey will have to take a rain check on that second cup of tea, we need to head out. There is still some stuff that we need to handle."

I can't believe what David just said. How can they just drop a huge bomb like this on her and then leave her to pick up the pieces by herself? I want to say something, but before I can, my mom speaks up.

"Can Hailey stay? Just for a little while. Y'all can go and take care of whatever y'all need to do, then come back and get her. I'd love to share some memories of Sam with her, I'm sure she loved him as much as he did her."

My gaze shifts between John and David, my heart racing as I anticipate their response. Wanting to spend any time that I can with my mom, even if its just an additional five minutes, I summon my best puppy dog eye face. I lower my lip into a pout, widen my eyes to appear as innocent as possible, and project a sense of longing that's lived within me for as long as I can remember. I'm not above using a bit of theatrics if it means gaining a few precious moments with my mom. John's resistance is the first to waver, his resolve breaking as a smile tugs at the corner of his lips. His eyes soften, reflecting affection and understanding. David however is a tough sell. Shaking his head slightly in a small 'no' aimed towards John, he gets a shrug of the shoulders in response. Still not budging, he tilts his head towards both of us in a motion to walk towards him as he leads us into the adjacent living room.

"I really don't think that's a good idea. We still don't know where the shooter is, and we need to keep her safe."

David hushed conversation with John carries an air of secrecy as if I'm not present in the room. Instead, I stand here feeling a bit frustrated by the exclusion, wondering why he brought me in here if he's not going to allow me to contribute to the discussion. I'm on the brink of saying something when John steps in, interjecting with a soft yet authoritative tone, redirecting the focus back to me.

"I get it. I do. But we can throw some wards up around the house here, and it will allow us to take care of the other one. We won't be that far away, and we can leave Hailey with a phone to call if they sense any trouble."

"I don't like it John."

"Well D, you don't have to like it. And if we're being honest, you and I both know that Hailey being back at that house while we clean up probably isn't the smartest idea either. She'll be safer here, where the shooter doesn't know where she is. Or would you rather he be at a house that's already been compromised?"

I can see it the moment that John's reasoning wins David over. The line between his eyebrows smoothing, and his jaw going slightly lax. Finally instead of talking about me, he turns slightly and talks to me, handing me his cell phone.

"Fine, but you heard John. Any sign of trouble at all, and you call us. Johns programmed as the second person in my favorites. Call, and we'll be here. I'm not kidding Hailey, if a bird chirps wrong, I want you calling us."

"Got it, yea okay."

As I watch David and my mom exchange a hug before he follows John out of the door, shaking his head as he locks it behind them. My gaze follows them as they walk towards the side of the house and disappear towards the back, and can't help but wonder what they are doing. My question is answered a few moments later when they reappear on the opposite side of the house. I can only guess that they are placing the wards that John mentioned earlier, as I watch their mouths move in unison, seemingly mimicking the same words. They finish back at the sidewalk, look back towards the house with a wave, and head towards the car.

With John and David departing, I turn my attention back to my mom who's immersed in cleaning the tea men's cups and offer my help as I make my way back towards the kitchen. Her polite decline doesn't surprise me; my mom has always been the nurturing type, wanting to take care of others even in times of uncertainty. I take a seat at the kitchen table, returning to my cup of tea, its warmth and familiarity offering a small comfort. As I sip from the cup, the flavors intertwine with memories of the shared moments that continue to flood my mind.

"So... uh... Miss—"

"You can call me Sarah. No miss needed."

The word "Miss" feels odd on my tongue, especially when what I truly want to call her is "mom." It's a surreal experience, sitting across from my mom yet feeling like a stranger in a home that is both familiar and different. I don't know if she knows what Sam was, or about the complexities of the world we live in. Given the cautious explanations provided by Sam and John, I think it's safe to assume that she might not be privy to the supernatural aspects of their lives. Not wanting to break any rules that might be unbeknownst to me, I keep up with the act.

"Right, Sarah. So how much did Sam tell you?"

"Um. I'm not sure. I think he told me everything, but that

could be just me assuming. He talked about when you and your aunt first got here, and that your parents had been in an accident. I'm sorry to hear that by the way." I nod as she continues. "He told me about your travels that your aunt took you on for your birthday each year and even showed me some pictures. He showed me pictures of when he first taught you to roller skate, and the time that you won a rodeo art contest. He really did talk about you all of the time, to the point that it felt like I knew you even though we had never met. When we first started dating, I thought that you were his daughter from the way he bragged about you, that's how you got the nickname of unofficial daughter."

God how I wish I could tell her everything. Heck, I wish him and I would have known everything. Her words give me a glimpse into the life I could have had if things had been different. Maybe I could have lived with them, we could have been a family. It angers me that we were deprived of the opportunity, and I wonder if my aunt knew about any of this.

***

Sarah and I have been talking for over an hour, our heartfelt conversation covering a broad range of subjects, all revolving around Sam. We've laughed, we've cried, and we've sat silent when words or emotions can't accurately describe how we feel. John has texted Davids phone a hand full of times checking on how we are, and I'd be willing to bet either David has put him up to it, or he's using John's phone to check in himself. The latest message informing us that they will be another half hour before returning.

After three more cups of hot tea, I excuse myself for another trip to the bathroom, this time going straight there and back. As I return from the bathroom and approach the living room, my senses are on high alert. I hear a male voice speaking, and my mind immediately starts racing with possibilities. Could it be John or David calling her, unable to get ahold of me in the two minutes that I was gone? Or is it someone else entirely? As I get closer moving trepidly towards the living room, my heart pounds in my chest. The unfamiliar voice becomes clearer, and I realize that it's not a voice I recognize from earlier conversations. Panic starts to bubble up within me as I reach the juncture of the hallway and the living room. Reaching for my phone, I realize that I've made a rookie mistake leaving it in the kitchen when I went to the bathroom. I spot my phone on the edge of the kitchen table, a few feet away, and I can practically feel the seconds ticking away in slow motion. My eyes dart around, trying to locate the source of the voice, but Sarah is no longer in the kitchen and the voice has abruptly stopped, leaving an eerie silence in its wake.

"Sarah?"

Getting no response in combination with the house completely quiet now, I wonder if she's walked outside to finish her phone call. Talking myself out of the panic that is beginning to overtake my senses, I know that if I can just get to my phone, I will feel better. Taking one more breath and holding it, I peak around the the corner to view the rest of the kitchen and most of the living room. Confident that no one is in the house, I let my breath out and begin to walk towards the table where my phone sits. My steps falter and my heart skips a beat as I hear a sudden thud, and then a searing pain radiates from the back of my head. It feels like the world spins for a moment, and my vision blurs as if I've been hit by a heavy blow. Panic and disorientation surge through me. Instinctively I bring my hands to the back of my head, and my vision threatens to give out when my fingers come away sticky and warm with blood.

I can feel my body being jolted around, my mouth is covered in a soft cloth and my wrists are being bound behind me by something I'm not quite sure of until the sound of a zip tie being pulled fills the air. My vision is hazy, and black dots float around the perimeters so that I'm not able to make out the person who has bound me until they finish and take a few steps back. Unable to run, I immediately begin to buck my body back and forth. Struggling against the restraints in an attempt to break the zip ties at my wrists, a wave of defeat washes over me when I realize that my ankles are tied too. The room swims into focus, and my eyes lock onto the menacing figure of the man who shot Sam, his smirk sending shivers down my spine. My efforts to break free come back with a vengeance as I watch him move towards the kitchen and drag Sarah's unconscious body into view. The sight of her limp form sends shock waves of horror through me as I scream through the cloth that covers my mouth. My throat raw with desperation, tears immediately fill my eyes. How can he do this? First he comes after me in Florida, then he kills Sam, and now Sarah? Why? Why didn't he just kill me when he had the chance? Why kill Sam and Sarah? Does he somehow know who they are? I want to scream and yell at him, hell I want to kill the bastard myself.

"Don't worry little bird, she's not dead. I would never do that to her."

I still instantly, not sure that I heard him correctly. Only one person has ever called me little bird, and there's no way that he could know that. My aunt gave me that nickname when we first moved here. I was so sad and rebellious those first few months, that I refused to eat. She joked that she had to hand feed me like a little bird. The nickname only made me that much angrier, doing what I'm sure she intended with some type of reverse psychology, that I'd end up eating my entire plate. So no, he couldn't know that name, or the meaning behind it unless some how he had taken her too. Had he? Is that why when I called out for her after Sam had been shot that she didn't come? Had he gotten into the house and taken her, or worse, killed her too? The rage inside me takes over any panic that I was feeling. Despite the pain, I continue to pull at the bindings with all the strength I can muster. Determined to make progress, a new dampness begins to pool at my wrists and the sound of his chilling laughter fills the room.

"I would tell you to stop, that you're only making yourself bleed. But you'll be bleeding a lot more by the time that I'm done with you."

His words cause my rage to turn into ice in my veins, and I begin to believe that I've only seen a glimpse of what he's capable of. I assumed that he would just shoot me like he did Sam. Take the easy way out, one and done, but something in his eyes tells me different. As he walks towards the kitchen, I maneuver myself to a seated position and try to scoot my way through the living room. My desperate attempt to reach my phone is cut short by the glint of a menacing blade in his hand as he rounds the corner back towards the living room.

Fear pulses through me like an electric shock, paralyzing me for a split second. The realization that he's armed with a knife, coupled with the cruel amusement in his eyes, sends shivers down my spine. My scream pierces the air, a mixture of terror and frustration, as I'm abruptly reminded of my helplessness. Every fiber of my being screams at me to run, to fight, to do anything to escape his clutches, but the reality of my restraints keep me rooted in place. His laughter, a haunting symphony of sadism, fills the room as he takes deliberate steps toward me.

"Oh this?" Holding the knife up up a little further, he twists it around, "This isn't for you. Well not yet... First things first."

Making his way past me and back into the living room, I look on in shock as he walks to where Sarah is sprawled on the floor. He bends down, his movements disturbingly casual, as if he's merely examining an object of curiosity. His fingers touch her skin, moving her head from side to side assessing her level of consciousness. I strain to catch any sign of life from Sarah, my breath caught in my throat as I try to gauge if she's awake or if she's fallen victim to the same fate as Sam. Her stillness is unnerving, and the weight of the unknown threatens to suffocate me.

"I'm sorry, but I have to do this."

Vomit threatens to explode from my mouth as he lifts the knife above his head, the sun pouring in from the windows reflecting on its clean blade. The knife descends, its trajectory deliberate and precise, as if he's done this countless times before. The sickening thud as the blade pierces her abdomen echoes in my ears. I can't move, can't scream, can't do anything when my mom doesn't even flinch at the puncture. I want to look away, but like a train wreck I can't as he pulls it back out in the same smooth motion that he shoved it in, its blade slick with the crimson evidence of his violence. A guttural sob tears its way from my throat, the sound raw and unfiltered while hot tears stream down my face once again, mingling with the dread that clutches at my heart.

"Why? Why?"

The defeated words are as muffled by the cloth still over my mouth, but the man that now stands over me must understand what I'm saying as a crooked smile breaks across his face.

"Why? Oh little bird, because of you. All of this is because of you."

Something about that phrase still sits wrong with me, a lingering unease amidst the emotions that engulf me. The weight of loss bears down on my chest as I'm reminded that on top of Sam, and now my mom, there's a good possibility that I've lost my aunt as well. I tilt my head slightly, my brows furrowing in a desperate attempt to communicate my confusion, hoping that he understands the plea in my quizzical expression. Even if he were to release the gag on my mouth, I doubt I would have the energy to ask.

My mind, already stretched to its limits by the horrors of this night, struggles to process the surreal scene playing out before me. A shimmer beings to illuminate the outline of this man. My heart begins to race, and I watch in a mix of disbelief and terror as his features begin to shift and contort, the shimmer enveloping his entire body like a cloak. Between one blink and the next, I go from looking at the man who shot

Sam to witnessing the impossible, my aunt standing in the exact same spot he once occupied. My immediate reaction is relief to seeing a friendly face, before my brain catches up to reality. The truth hits like a sledgehammer to my gut, the realization that David was right. The laugh that emanates from her lips shatters any remnants of my fleeting relief, sending a shiver of pure dread down my spine.

# 20

# Kat

"I told you little bird, the only thing that I wanted, was to save my best friend. At first, I tried to save you both. I thought that she would be lost without you. But after what felt like the hundredth try, I realized that you are the problem."

I can sense Hailey's confusion and bewilderment, her eyes reflecting a mix of disbelief and fear as she tries to unravel the incomprehensible reality before her. I watch as she struggles to reconcile the two seemingly contradictory versions of me; the loving aunt who took her in and protected her, and the man who materialized in her Florida room with a sinister agenda. I can't blame her for her confusion. The situation has spiraled into something far beyond what I had anticipated. It wasn't supposed to be me standing over her right now. I had it all planned out perfectly until last nights shit show went down.

"That's right Hailey. This isn't the first time we've done

this. Hell it's not even the fifth time that we've done it. You see, the first time I saved you I thought that I could go back for her. I didn't realize that your lack of active powers would tether me to the same restrictions of time travel that you have, and I was unable to go back for her. Then you ended up getting sick and dying before time could catch back up to itself. The second time I traveled too far back in time and your powers became active before time caught up to itself. You went in search of her, and she got killed in the crossfire when that timeline of you was a year old... So I killed the older you and took the one year old back a few years. Another time, David accidentally killed her, trying to kill me, to save you. Well, not me, but another version of me." To prove my point, I morph into a blonde hair green eyed woman before changing back into the person that Hailey knows and loves as her Aunt. "Anyway, you get the point. Every time I tried to save her, it didn't work out for one reason or another. But this last time. This last time I figured it out. It's you."

I think back on the countless instances where I've tried to mend the past, to rewrite the events. All of the things that worked, while others unraveled in unexpected ways, all rooted in my initial actions that set the dominoes in motion. I understand the saying that hindsight is twenty twenty, and even though this time hasn't worked out exactly as I planned for it to, it still managed to get me to the ending that I needed. I remember the frustration that washed over me when my initial plan in Florida faltered. I had placed my trust in an accomplice who couldn't execute a single task correctly, prompting me to devise a contingency plan. In my mind, it should have been straightforward: a straightforward kidnapping, controlled and orchestrated. I had kept Sam busy and supplied him the means to sedate Hailey, ensuring a smooth transition without struggle. But that, too, veered off course. At first, I was livid, but when David is the one who was there after the fire, I knew that I was getting closer. He didn't recognize me of course, but I knew who he was instantly. The shift in the dynamic of knowledge favored me, allowing me to exist in different forms while retaining my memories, while he struggled to reassemble the puzzle each new iteration. Sam and Sarah's timeline has been forever changing, altering courses with each cycle, making it incredibly hard for me to track them down in a consistent pattern. I was worried that they would somehow miss the opportunity of meeting when Sam suggested that he wanted to move to Louisiana, and for us to come with him, so I pushed back for as long as I could. But with the clock ticking closer and closer to Hailey's conception, I finally gave in, trusting that the intricacies of fate would guide us toward the inevitable. Then when John showed up at the house, I thought that everything would prematurely explode. I thought that when she heard his voice in the car and couldn't place it, that we were in the clear, that she didn't remember him. But when he came in the door that day, even before she spoke the words her face told me that she recognized him, and that she wasn't going to be quite about it. Her recognition of him threatened to unravel all that I had worked for and I knew I had to do something, but I wasn't sure what. Before I was able to come up with with a clear and concise plan, David arrived presenting an opportunity that was as risky as it was promising. I transformed into my male form, grabbed the gun I keep out of my nightstand and slipped out of the back window. As the gunshot shattered the air yesterday, the trajectory of the bullet went awry, missing its intended target. I was aiming for David. Finally this was going to be my opportunity to take him out, one less person that would be looking out for Hailey when the time came. But then Sam and David moved at the last second, sliding in opposite directions, and the bullet found Sam instead. I knew that David could move at super sonic speed, and couldn't take the risk of being caught, so I hightailed it out of there hoping he wouldn't come chasing.

The implications of that moment ricocheted in ways I hadn't foreseen, and now, with Hailey before me, her pulse weakening, the threads of time seem to converge. I can tell that she is trying to pay attention, but her eyes aren't tracking quite the way that they should and are starting to become glossed over. Kneeling beside her, my fingers pressing against the rhythm of her pulse, I can feel the cadence slowing beneath my touch. The anticipation thrills me, the culmination of my efforts within my grasp, my plan finally coming to fruition.

"You're feeling it, aren't you? Can you feel your heart slowing down? It's going to work this time!"

The chime of Davids phone dings on the table drawing my attention and stirring a pang of anxiousness within my chest. Picking it I keep my face a mask of calculated neutrality as I read the text displayed on the screen as to not give Hailey any indication of just how close David and John are. I'm grateful that David's phone lacks a lock screen, a small detail that works in my favor as I move my fingers swiftly over the screen composing a response letting them know all is well. If him or John think that Hailey is texting, maybe they won't think there is any reason to rush back.

"Well, looks like we are going to have to speed this up a bit. I wasn't sure if this would work and wanted to watch it all play out. You know, stabbing her in the stomach so that she bleeds out just enough to lose the baby she's carrying. You're directly linked to it, since it's you, and theoretically if the fetus no longer exists, you shouldn't either. But, David and John will eventually come back, and I need to make sure that neither the future you or the past you exist. You see, that's what I finally figured out, you both have to die. If neither of you exist, then no one will come looking for you, and she will never die. We will finally be free from this dreadful cycle."

Getting a little emotional, I feel hope that for the first time, my plan will finally pan out. The faint stirring of tears pricks at the corners of my eyes, and is a sensation that I surprisingly welcome. It's as if this moment carries the weight of all my previous failures, and the prospect of success feels more possible than ever. I have a weird urge to thank her for some reason. For her sacrifice? For finally being able to keep Sarah alive? I'm not sure, so instead I settle for a silent hug.

"Goodbye little bird"

The words escape my lips as a hushed, barely audible even in the profound silence that envelopes us. As I release her from my embrace, I commit to the final act of my plan. My grip tightens around the knife's handle, and with a swift, controlled motion, I drive it deep into her chest. Its surprisingly harder than one would think, the resistance of bones pushing back at me before the resounding crunch of them giving way. Hesitating for a moment, wondering if I should leave it in, twist it around, or yank it back out I catch a gimps of Hailey's face. Her eyes are wide with a silent terror and tears free flow down them, and I find myself taken aback that there was no screaming. I thought that this might be a loud drawn out thing, but instead its almost as if the act itself has stolen the breath from her lungs. Deciding that the stab alone is enough, and not wanting to leave the murder weapon, I pull the knife back out in the same manner that it was plunged in, swift, fast and unforgiving. Unable to continue to hold herself up, I step back and watch as Hailey immediately falls to the side, her energy palpable has it seeps from the gaping wound in her chest. Her blood runs freely and I step back, careful to avoid any incriminating prints or bloodstains on my shoes while the pooling crimson paints the floor beneath her. I watch for a moment as the life begins to leave her eyes. Walking over to Sarah, who is still unconscious I check for a strong pulse and can't help but to smile knowing that this time will finally be the time.

The sound of a car door draws my attention, and I pivot towards the front windows, catching sight of John as he approaches, David following suit. Transforming back into the man who had shot Sam to conceal my identity, I turn towards the back of the house and run out of the back door. Taking a chance and pausing in the yard, I conceal my presence from their view by positioning myself in the shadows cast by a bookcase that partially obscures the window. With tension gripping my every movement, I watch through it as everything unfolds. John is the first through the door, with David right on his heels, both men stopping dead in their tracks taking in the scene.

"Fuck... fuck! What do we do?"

John rushes over to Hailey, holding her in his arms, a low hum emanating from him. Is this what he does? A mixture of frustration and unease surges within me as I piece together the nature of his power, his ability to heal. I want to run back in there and plow into him, keeping him from helping her. I want to yell at him to stop, to demand he attend to Sarah instead. My hands clench involuntarily, fingernails digging into my palms, the temptation to intervene almost unbearable. Knowing that I can't risk blowing my cover, it takes every ounce of my being to force myself to stay where I am. Minutes stretch into eternity as John keeps his energy focused on Hailey, her lifeless body sprawled in a pool of blood that continues to expand around her. In a moment that I began to doubt would ever come, David finally steps forward, his voice slicing through the air, breaking the silence.

"Leave her John. It's too late for her. Come help Sarah."

"What? No, I can't! I can't just leave her D, she's dying!"

"Let her go John. You're going to have to trust me on this. I know you haven't been here before, but I have. You need to let her go and save Sarah. We'll get her next time."

"Next time? What do you mean next time?"

John's voice emerges hoarse and heavy, and I can tell he's reluctant to let Hailey go. David must notice the same reluctance that I do as he walks over to him, his hand landing on John's shoulder. No verbal exchange transpires, yet an unspoken understanding seems to pass between them. A breath of a second later the humming slows to a halt, and I watch as John's arms slip away from her mumbling 'I'm sorry' over and over. With David's support, John manages to regain his footing, his unsteady steps directed away from Hailey towards Sarah. As the hum from before begins again David crosses the room and retrieves his phone from the table, his voice steady as he gives the address and a brief visual of the scene to a 911 operator. I want to stay and watch the rest unfold, make sure that Sarah is okay, but I know that I need to get out of here before David begins walking around looking for signs of the perpetrator. Now that I know where Sarah is, it will be easy for me to keep tabs on her and track her down again once she's recovered. Prying my gaze away from the scene, every step toward the back of the house feels like a reluctant retreat, as I hop the neighbors fence and head in the direction of my parked car.

# 21

# Epilogue

The beeping of machines is the first thing that I notice as I wake up, and briefly wonder if I've set some weird alarm on my phone. An involuntary groan escapes my lips as I attempt to shift to find the source of the obscenity, only to be met by a searing pang in my abdomen. The sensation forces my eyes open, revealing the sterile environment of a hospital room. In an instant, the fog lifts and memories rush back with brutal clarity. The news of Sam's death from John, David, and Hailey's visit. The countless cups of tea Hailey and I reminisced over memories of Sam. The gas utility man knocking on the door claiming a leak had been reported, and requesting to inspect our stove and furnace. Me walking him into the kitchen, showing him where the stove was. His ungodly grip on the back of my hair as I walked away and slamming my head down onto the unforgiving granite counter top. Panic surges through me as I realize that Hailey was in the house when this happened, yet she's not here in the room with me. An alarm begins to sound as I tear off the monitoring wires that are strapped to my checks and the clamp around my finger. I'm debating on pulling out the IV in my arm, or taking the bags with me to find someone, when a woman in green scrubs bursts through the door., her gaze shifting between me and the disrupted

"Ma'am! Ma'am, you're okay! Look at me, you're okay. Take a deep breath and calm down."

I don't realize that I'm holding my breath already until I try to take another. Letting it out, and sucking another in, I try to get up and move past her.

"Please ma'am, stay in the bed. You've been in an accident and have been out for a few days. You lost a lot of blood and are going to be weak, I don't want the stitches on your stomach to tear or for you to fall. Just sit back down and I'll page a doctor."

Reluctantly, I comply with her directions, easing myself back onto the bed as she deftly reattaches the same wires that I had so hastily torn from my chest. Annoyed, but knowing an attitude won't get me anywhere, I put on my sweet face and hope for the best.

"My phone? Do you know where it is?"

"I'm sorry ma'am, you didn't come with any belongings. Your brother visits you a few times a day though, and I'm sure that he can bring it to you when he comes back by this afternoon."

"My brother?"

"Yes, I think he said his name was James?"

"John?"

"Yes that's him. He usually comes by in the morning, around lunch, and again around shift change in the evenings. You've got about an hour or two before his lunch time appearance, but I can call him if you'd like me to, let him know you're awake."

I nod in agreement, my voice laced with gratitude as I express how much I would appreciate her help. I can't help but be in awe at John's fast thinking though. He must have known that they wouldn't let him see me or give him updates on my condition if he wasn't related. The nurse finishes reattaching me to the monitors, managing to only give me the side eye of annoyance once, before putting a call into who I'm assuming the is the doctor, to tell them I'm up.

"The rounding doctor is dealing with an emergency right now, but an attending will be by soon to answer any questions."

"Do you know if a girl was brought in with me?"

"I'm sorry, but again, the attending will have to answer any questions."

The nurse's expression, though guarded, provides me with more insight than her words, and I know without pushing any further that Hailey was brought in, and that it doesn't look good.

I can't shake the anxiousness that courses through me as I sit there, watching the clock as thirty minutes tick by at an agonizingly slow rate. My first instinct is to reach out to John, but I don't have his number memorized. I try calling Sam's phone instead, hoping John has it, but it goes straight to voicemail. Trying my own phone next, it rings for what feels like an eternity before finally being sent to voicemail as well. Agitated and not wanting to wait around any longer, I start looking for a way to disconnect myself without setting off the alarms again. The IV poll next to my bed rolls, and I'm just about to say forget it and rip off the wires again when the room door swings open and a young man in a white coat strides in.

"Well, it sure is nice to see you up."

Realizing I've been caught, I can't help but feel a bit embarrassed as I awkwardly shift back into the divot I've made in the mattress. His voice carries a professional calmness as he goes through a concise list of my injuries, seemingly surprised that I've managed to escape with just a concussion and a single stab wound to the abdomen. The word "miracle" slips from his lips and I don't understand why he would consider it that until I realize that maybe Hailey wasn't so lucky.

"The young girl, the one that was brought in with me."

I take a shot in the dark, acting like I know for a fact she was brought here. To my relief, my gamble pays off as the doctor's demeanor undergoes a swift transformation. The cheerful storytelling of my survival gives way to a somber cloud of sadness that is palpable across the room and it becomes painfully evident that my suspicions from earlier are right.

"I'm sorry ma'am. But unfortunately your nieces injuries were catastrophic, there was nothing that we could do. EMS attempted to resuscitate, but the location and nature of the injury was just too much. She passed before making it to the hospital."

The wave of emotions crashes over me, threatening to drown my thoughts. I want to cry, for Sam, and for Hailey who's young life taken too soon. And for what? Sam's death was a freak accident, but Hailey... He could have left her alone. She was just a kid for Christ's sake. The realization gnaws at me, fueled by anger at the unfairness of it all. I should have known. I should have known when I gave up my immortality in heaven for love, choosing to live my life out as a fallen angel on earth, that there would be a catch. The universe never gives without taking and we are constantly reminded of the checks and balance. Frustration with my own blindness replaces my tears, leaving me numbed to the core as the doctor's request to examine me fades into the background. Succumbing to the numbness, I don't feel it has his stethoscope presses against my chest. As he instructs me to follow a light with my eyes, my attention drifts away, consumed by my inner turmoil. His words become even more distant as he asks me to lift my gown so he can assess the laceration on my stomach. Gritting my teeth as he pokes and prods around the tender spot, my universe comes to a halt at his next revelation.

"I'm sorry can you repeat that please?"

"Oh, yes, sure. I was just saying that we did have to give you a few units of blood, and it was touch and go for a moment there, but as of right now, you and you're baby are fine. We'll continue to monitor your blood work, and refer you to a high risk OB-GYN due to the scar tissue that might form along your uterus, but we're hopeful.

"I'm.... I'm pregnant?"

"Um.... yes."

I stare blankly as he flips through my chart, still not certain that I'm hearing him correctly.

"Yep. By the levels of your HGC, I'd say about four weeks.

It's still very early on, but your levels are continuing to rise, so that's a good sign. Looks like your baby is just as much of a fighter as you."

My mind is a haze as he continues to speak, his words a distant murmur in my ears. I'm too consumed by my thoughts to fully comprehend his explanations. A soft knock at the door jolts me back to reality, and as Johns familiar face peaks around it I burst into tears. Seeing him brings me a sense of relief, knowing that I'm not alone. But him coming alone also solidifies everything that's happened. Sam and Hailey are gone, and I could have died too. The Dr. takes the cue, excusing himself to give us some privacy leaving John and I in the room alone. Time stretches, marked by the clicks of the second hand on the wall clock. Fifty-four seconds go by before we both speak at the same time.

"So—"

"I'm pregnant."

I let him chew on that for a moment, and I have to give him credit for how fast he makes a comeback.

"Wow, I mean... wow. How do you feel?

"Sad, scared, excited. I don't know, I just found out and I'm feeling all of the emotions right now."

"Yea. Yea I get that. Well congrats I guess, right? I mean, I'm not really sure what to say here."

"No, no, yea congratulations is okay. We've lost so much already, you know? Maybe this is the universes' way of trying to make it right."

"That's a good way to look at it. Yea, I like that."

"If it's a boy, I'm going to name it after Sam. Let him be

his fathers namesake. It's the least I could do, you know? Pass down his dad's name to him."

"What if it's a girl?"

I don't even have to think about it. It's the only name that seems right given everything that happened and how important she was to him.

"Hailey. I'd name her Hailey."

www.ingramcontent.com/pod-product-compliance
Ingram Content Group UK Ltd.
Pitfield, Milton Keynes, MK11 3LW, UK
UKHW040006200726
13854UKWH00001B/66